The Island
on the Edge
of Normal

by
Guy New York

The Island
on the Edge
of Normal

by
Guy New York

QNY

The Island on the Edge of Normal

Copyright © 2012 by Guy New York

2012

ISBN 978-0615728476

QNY
907 Broadway
New York, NY 10010
www.quickienewyork.com

For Laura Beth,
the love of my life.

Chapter One

From Boston I took a long slow bus ride up the coast, through New Hampshire and into Maine. I watched the ocean with wide eyes, realizing it had been years since I had seen it. I lived so close to the water, with New York's harbor spilling out into the Atlantic, but I never once made it so far as Coney Island. In fact, I had barely left Manhattan in the last twelve months. Compared to the city, the ocean felt vast and alone in ways I never imagined.

I got off in a small port town where a ferry took passengers to a few of the islands. Paul was standing outside a coffee shop waiting for me. He was smoking a cigarette and drinking a cup of coffee. His face was lined from the sun and he looked more relaxed than I knew was possible.

We walked from the bus stop down the quiet streets to the ferry dock and then out onto the boat. It was a crisp, cool night, and for the first time in years I looked up to see stars. They shone brightly overhead, reminding me instantly that I was no longer home. I could see the entire Milky Way above me, and I almost fell over as I craned my neck and got lost in the lights.

"Remind me how you know Stephanie?" Paul asked as we found a spot at the front rail.

"She was my roommate's girlfriend my freshman year of college. She practically lived in our room for six months, and we used to play poker until four in the morning."

"That's fantastic. I haven't seen her in a long time, but it was nice to get her phone call. She tells me you're a writer."

"Yup. How about you?" I wanted to tell him I used to be a writer, and I wanted to tell him just why I was here, but I couldn't find the words. I felt silly and young, and the cold breeze off the water almost made it feel as if it didn't matter at all.

"Wine," he said quietly. "My company distributes wine, mostly from the West Coast, and we sell and promote it here in New England. I hope you drink it, because Issa and I live on the stuff. I brought a few bottles home that we can try tomorrow. It'll be a little welcome treat."

"That sounds fantastic. I don't know a damn thing about wine, but I'm excited to learn. How long have you lived here?" The boat slipped out through the bay and into open water.

"My aunt and uncle owned the house, and when my uncle died, Stephen and I moved up to help out. He's my kid from my first wife. The aunt was a crazy old lady, and she drove us nuts, but we fell in love with the place all the same. The island held us here, and after she passed away eight years ago, we didn't even talk about leaving. It's quiet, and pretty, and sometimes I think the ocean won't let us go."

We were quiet, and Paul's ease let the silence just be. We stood and watched the waves as the ferry moved through the night air, and I felt far away and completely unsure of everything.

The trip was lovely, and the sea was calm and quiet. An hour went by before we arrived in a small village on the north side of an island. I could see lights shining along the rocky shore, but all I could hear was the quiet noise of the ferry engine as we slid into the landing dock. The air on the island was warmer than I expected and the night breeze felt good as we walked down the plank.

It was hard to make out details in the dark, but the town was small and spread out along the rocky shoreline. There were two bicycles at the end of the wharf that Paul and his son had left in the morning. Stephen had walked home, so I had the pleasure of riding across the island with Paul; my suitcase was balanced precariously in front of me, and I felt ridiculous and alive.

When we arrived at the house the lights were off and all was quiet. Paul showed me to the extra room, where the bed was already made. The walls were mostly bare, except for one large poster I could barely make out by the dim light of the moon shining in the window. I could just see the shape of the New York City skyline in the moonlight, and I felt like I was even farther away. Paul said goodnight as he slipped back out into the hallway, and I was alone for the first time in ages.

I sat down on the bed and stared out the window. I closed my eyes and opened them again. I breathed the cold air and rubbed the warm blankets with the palm of my hand, and I was suddenly aware of something new. I wanted to write. Or at least I wanted to want to write. It had been a year since I put a single word down, and if I didn't start I was pretty sure that I might never.

Excited, I sat down on a small chair that looked out the dark window. I pulled the pen from my pocket and tried to find words. All that came to mind were memories of city streets and diners, Jane, our apartment. There was nothing at all of where I was, and nothing at all that felt like the sea.

I finally pulled out Jane's old letter and wondered what it would be like to light it on fire and let it flame out over the waves. I unfolded it and skimmed through it again as I struggled not to get lost. Jane and I reserved paper letters for when we had something dirty to say, and this one was no exception. Even when we moved in together we mailed them, and the waiting was part of the fun. Each one got more and more outrageous until sometimes it was hard to tell what was simply fantasy and what we might actually do.

I skimmed through it until I found the part I remembered best. It was a game that led to more sleepless nights than I could remember.

I want you to drive me crazy with jealousy tonight. I want to hear things I don't ever want to hear, and I want you to make me beg until I cry.

I want to know how tight she was and when you fuck me I want you to call me her name. I want you to tell me you love her more and you want her more than me. Make me scream and cry until I can't hold on, and then keep going. Push me further and further until I beg you to stop, and then make me come until I'm blind in both eyes.

Come on me and in me, and leave scratches down my body that I'll have for days. Don't let me forget that I'm yours.

I read it again and all those nights came flooding back to me. For the first time in a year I wanted her next to me whispering terrible things in my ear. I wanted to hold her tightly and I wanted to hear her beg. I folded and unfolded the letter a few more times and finally slipped it into my bedside table.

Chapter Two

I awoke to the smell of rich New England coffee and it stirred me from bed more quickly than normal. I found my three hosts sitting around the table eating a breakfast of warm bread, cheese, and fruit. Paul motioned to the coffee pot on the stove, and I slid over and poured myself a cup before anyone else noticed me.

"Hey James, did you sleep well?" Stephen asked when he looked up from his book. He managed to get the question out just as the coffee touched my lips, and it took me a second until I could tell him that yes indeed, I had slept excellently, and I couldn't be happier to be here.

"Do you take anything in your coffee?" Paul asked.

"It's delicious just as it is," I replied. It was almost too bitter for me, but it tasted nothing like one of Suzanne's lattes, so I was content.

I took the only empty seat. Paul's wife, her eyes bright green and her red hair a messy tangle on top of her head, leaned over and said, "I'm Melissa, but you can call me Issa. Everyone else does."

"It's nice to meet you," I said, offering her a hand.

She shook my hand with a firm grip.

"And it's nice to meet you too, James. But you can relax, we're not that formal out here. That said, we are glad you're here. The porch needs painting, the garden is a terrible mess, and..."

"Let's give him a day or two before we put him to work,

dear," Paul interrupted with a warm smile.

We chatted and ate our breakfast slowly until Paul and Stephen had to head out the door to catch the ferry. Paul's office was on the mainland, and Stephen had school for another two weeks.

Issa and I sat there silently enjoying what was left of breakfast, and I took a moment to look around. Between the kitchen and the living room was a counter where we sat eating breakfast. It was an island in an island, and from where I sat I could see the front of the house was open and spacious. There were enough large windows to let in the warmth of the sun and the smell of the sea. The living room was filled by two low couches and a huge chair that in my apartment would have been so full of pretzels and change that you couldn't sit down. The walls were speckled white, and the brown wood of the window frames matched the rough floorboards. A piano stood against one wall, weathered and colored from the humidity blowing in, and on the far wall was a fireplace. The windows themselves opened up onto rocky fields in the south and the descending shoreline on the west side of the house. All in all, it was small and comfortable.

"I like your pajamas," Issa said, looking over at me.

She had her knees tucked up and sat on her chair looking like a child even though she was years older than me. I had on warm flannel plaids and I felt like an out-of-place lumberjack or a Brooklyn hipster at a sleepover. Her smile was infectious, though, and I was pretty sure I could look at her all day long and never get tired of it.

"I thought flannel might make sense for Maine. Guess I was wrong."

"It's not exactly Alaska, but it sometimes gets cold at night. You'll be glad you brought them."

I got up when I was finished, insisting that Issa drink her coffee while I did the dishes. She was quiet as she watched my hands in the soapy water. The chore felt grounding as I worked without thinking. The house was new, the island unfamiliar, and Issa was perched like a cat on the edge of her chair with a smile that looked even further away. She sipped her coffee and fumbled with the last of the fruit.

"What do you do out here when they're off island?" I asked, looking over my shoulder.

"I'm an artist. Okay, I make pots. But it's like being an artist. I have a studio next to the porch, and I spend most of my day out there playing with clay. When I'm not fixing things, that is. Have you ever lived in an old house? You have no idea how often things break. It's almost a full-time job."

"As far I know, potters are artists. I'd love to see your work. As for the house, I'm not the biggest handyman in the world, but I'm happy to help however I can."

"Well, sometimes I feel like I'm too practical to make art, but you're washing one of mine now. And I do like fixing things, but I still need all the help I can get."

The mug in my hand was small and beautiful. It had no handle, but it was pleasing to hold and it warmed my body. It was deep blue with speckles of white that reminded me of the sea.

"I love it," I said.

I finished washing the dishes and started drying them off. Issa got up and showed me where everything went, and whenever her arm brushed against me I smiled and pulled away.

When everything was finished, I suddenly realized I had no idea what I was supposed to do. I should be writing something, or doing something, but all I wanted was to fall down onto the couch and finish my coffee.

"I'm going to get some work done, but I'll see you at lunch, okay?"

She walked down the hall, in her own flannel pajamas and

just before she slipped into her studio she turned and gave me a shy smile.

"James, I'm glad you're here."

And then she was gone, and I was alone in a stranger's house on an island in the middle of nowhere. I poured myself another cup of coffee, opened a window in the living room, and settled into the big chair. The breeze was cold as I wrapped myself in a blanket and looked out over the ocean. Here I am, I thought. Here is my beginning.

As I sat there, that first day, with a belly full of breakfast and black coffee still pouring down my throat, I felt almost at peace. The dishes were clean and put away, the table was cleared, and the quietness of the house was soothing. It was just what I hoped it would be, and yet nothing had changed. I was more lonely than ever, hours away from anyone I knew. I had everything a writer should need to create, and I was just as stuck as I had been in New York.

Chapter Three

That afternoon I began to wander the island. I found so many breaks in the shoreline and strange grottos buried in the rocks that I was sure Blackbeard must have taken port. The wind and the water had shaped the stone for secret love affairs and buried treasure, and there were dozens of ideal places to write. I marked each in my mind as I passed them by, and I got so lost that it took me hours to find my way back into town.

The next thing I discovered made me happier than I had been in ages. Right against the water was an idyllic little café. There were small tables outside on the patio, and a view of the harbor that couldn't be beat. The wood siding of the old house was weathered to perfection, and it felt more like Maine every second. I sat down and looked over the menu as I tried to rub the soreness out of my legs. Four hours of walking on rocky beaches was not something I was used to.

"You must be James," came a voice, startling me out of my daydream.

There was a woman standing next to me. She wore an apron and her long white hair was tightly pulled back. Her skin was tanned from the sun and her eyes were nearly gray. She looked timeless and had such a heavy New England accent I almost didn't understand her.

"This must be a small town," I said looking up.

"Small town. Small island. Hell, it's small world if you think about it. I'm Abigail, and this is my place," she said, offering a hand. I took it, and almost instantly regretted it. Her grip was like iron, and I tried not to cringe when she finally let go.

"What can I get you? We have a good cup of coffee and some of the best pie in the world. Some sharp cheddar and apple pie is our most popular." Except what Abigail actually said was "some shahp cheddah" and I loved every syllable of it.

"Sounds like I can't miss that."

Three minutes later she returned with the pie and the coffee, and before I could say a thing she sat down next to me at the table and put her feet up. So much for eating alone.

"So, New York," she said, as I took my first bite.

"Yup," I mumbled. The cold, sweet pie was followed by the strongest damn cheddar cheese I had ever tasted in my life. She was right, though. It was the perfect combination.

"What did you do there?"

I took a deep breath and said something I hadn't said in a long time:

"I'm a writer."

"Did you ever go to the White Horse Tavern?" she asked. "Dylan Thomas died there."

"Technically he died at the Chelsea Hotel, but he had his last drink at the White Horse." I'm not much of a history nerd, but there are a few things I do remember, even if it was just from reading the plaque at the bar.

"What's it like?" Her eyes got big as she leaned forward in her chair.

"It's an old bar full of old men and expensive cheeseburgers. But it does feel like New York. It's dark and it smells like wood and beer, and people talk to you whether you like it or not. It gets crowded on weekend nights, but it's nice on a rainy Sunday afternoon. I like it."

"I loved Dylan Thomas as a child. My father used to read him to me, and I would sit and listen as I tried to stay awake. Did you write there?"

"I can't write in bars. I've tried and I've tried but it just doesn't work. I drink beer and talk to strangers, and I forget what I was going to do as soon as I sit down."

"Well, you'll write here, I guess. It's wicked quiet during the day, and I'll tell my kids not to bother you."

"Kids?"

"You know, the kids who work here. If you work here, you work for Aunt Abigail."

She got up and patted me on the shoulder as she turned to walk back into the café. I took another bite of my pie and cheese before I was nearly hit by a seagull swooping by to pick up a scrap off the patio floor.

Abigail soon returned and sat down once more, topping off my coffee along with her own.

"So, are you a friend of Paul or Issa?"

"Neither. I mean, not yet. I'm an old friend of Paul's niece. I just met them. They're putting me up for a while until I can find someplace else."

Abigail blushed for a moment, and it was like watching stone change color in front of my eyes. She adjusted herself in her chair and nodded four or five times in a row.

"Well, that makes sense. I thought you might, ah, be here to see one of them in particular."

She got up quickly and picked up the plates from my table without saying another word. Just before she reached the door I called out for the check.

"Oh, the first one is on us. That's how we get ya hooked." She threw a smile over her shoulder and then she was gone.

I looked around the café and for a moment I thought she was right. I could write there. There were a few tourists coming and going, but it was so quiet I wondered how it survived.

I pulled my notebook out from my bag and opened it on the table in front of me. I thought about the White Horse and dark beer. I remembered taking Jane there one night on a date and how I regretted it almost instantly. Her face was skeptical and alert as she eyed the bartender, and I don't think we even made it through one round.

"Maybe if you write it down, I'd like it better," she told me. "But right now, it smells like stale beer and sweat."

The images came back, but my hand didn't move. I stared at the blank page. Every time I tried to start something held me back. I finally put the notebook away, finished my coffee, and started the long walk back to the house. I took slow breaths as I followed the path across the island, reminding myself over and over again that it was okay.

That evening, after dinner, the four of us sat out on the porch sipping wine and talking. It was crisp and cool, but the porch was screened in and the chairs were piled high with blankets. Small lanterns were the only light, and I felt like I was in a movie.

"So, what am I drinking?" I asked Paul as I picked up my glass. I could tell you everything there was to know about craft beer, Hudson Valley whiskeys, and peaty single malts, but wine was something I had managed to avoid.

"This is a Pinot noir from the Willamette Valley in Oregon. They're growing some of the best Pinot's out there, and this is one of my favorites. It has a nice medium body with hints of cherry and raspberry."

"Or, as I like to say, it's a yummy red from the Left Coast," Issa added.

"Am I supposed to taste it a certain way?"

"If you're like Paul and Issa you just gulp it down and then refill your glass. It's the Maine way of drinking wine. Up here you get worried it might freeze if you don't drink it quickly enough." Stephen was sitting on the couch with a mug of hot chocolate, and he had his feet up on the coffee table. His hair mostly covered his eyes, but even through his tangle of curls I could see a mischievous glint. I was going to have to watch out for that one.

"I'll keep that in mind," I said as Paul raised his glass in a toast. All four of us clinked our cups and the wine was delicious. I couldn't discern any raspberry, but it was light and tasty, and didn't remind me of my former life at all.

"So, are you going to write about us?" Stephen asked.

"Oh God no," I said a bit too quickly. "I mean, I'm not writing about anyone. It's fiction. I don't write about people I know."

"Man, I was hoping we'd get to be in a story. Maybe a creepy story where a deranged lobsterman comes out of the water at night and plays our piano in the dark to wake up his lost mermaid bride."

"That's actually a good idea. Mind if I steal it?"

"All my ideas are free. It's one of the first things they teach you in high school. Kids' thoughts are worth exactly nothing."

"Ouch," Paul said, as he pulled a cigarette from the box on the table.

"It's not that bad, but you know what I mean. We're supposed to figure out what other people think, not have our own thoughts. It's what modern education is all about."

"I don't think I envy your teachers," I said.

"Yeah, neither do they."

"So, James, what's your story? Stephanie says you're a writer and Issa says you're a good dishwasher." Paul leaned back in his chair as he blew smoke out through his nose.

"Up until yesterday I was a bartender and a house painter. Before that I was a writer, and before that I was a poor college student."

"How do you go from poor student to a writer just like that? I always think of writers as imaginary. I mean, I know people do it, but I don't understand how you make a living at it."

"For some reason a publisher decided it was a good idea to give me a contract right out of college. Something about being up and coming. And my parents thought it was enough of a success to keep funding me. Some people are artists, and some people are patrons. And some of us are just freeloaders."

Paul poured us another round of wine and for a moment I thought there would be more. I waited with my teeth clenched for a grilling that never came. Instead, Stephen went off to his room with a nod and a mumble, and Issa and Paul moved on to other things. I took a deep breath and let it out slowly. It was going to take time getting used to this.

An hour later they excused themselves, leaving the porch to find the comfort of their bed. I found myself wondering about my hosts and realizing that I knew almost nothing about them. They were warm and kind, and they welcomed me into their house for reasons I didn't quite understand. They were relaxed and content, and they didn't appear to struggle at all. They were Maine and I was New York. That wasn't going to work at all. I couldn't write as an anthropologist, sticking his nose in where he doesn't belong. I couldn't just watch and expect words to come.

Somewhat frustrated and confused, I picked myself up and made my way to the back door. I thought a walk might help clear my mind and hopefully when I returned I'd be able to focus on where I was rather than where I had been. I walked out the door and down through a patch of purple flowers scattered among the rocks. When I reached the edge of the water, I sat down behind a small ledge to block my view of the house. It was only an image in the dark, small and unobtrusive, but I wanted to find the real island. I wanted to find a place that could be nowhere else so I could do what I was supposed to do.

I took out my notebook once again, and this time I managed not to think. I didn't question myself or ask what I was doing. I opened to a clear blank page and I put my pen down against it.

One day in second grade my teacher asks me what I want to be when I grow up. I tell her that I want to be a writer. When she asks me why I tell her that I like the sound of typewriter keys. Don't be ridiculous, she says to me, that's a terrible reason to want to do something. She tells me I have to pick something else so I tell her I want to take pictures like my father instead.

Most likely this is a total invention, but I've heard it so many times that it's a part of my history. It's funny how that happens. It's a story my mother began telling when I was in high school and I started entering poetry competitions. She told it with an embarrassed sense of pride as if she wasn't sure if I was brilliant or possibly slow. Some days it encouraged me and I believed that I was a romantic from the time I was six, and other times it made me feel foolish. I'd roll my eyes when she started to tell the story or I'd walk out of the room so I didn't have to explain.

I still like the sound of typewriter keys. Maybe it's because of the story.

I wrote four pages and then tore them out of the notebook. Without thinking, I reached into my pocket and felt the cold metal of something square. I pulled out the Zippo, flipped open the lid, and was surprised when it lit easily in the cold wind coming off the water. I watched the flame before slowly moving the first page toward it until a corner caught. I watched it burn as I closed the lighter with my thumb. I held the second page to the first just as the flame was dying out, and I watched it too burn down until just a corner remained. The next two pages followed course, and soon I was standing on the beach while the ashes at my feet were blown out over the waves and the rocky shore.

I sat back against the cold rock and stared out at the sea, wondering what lay on the other side. As my life floated away I tucked my hands into my pockets to keep them warm. Everything I knew was gone.

I looked up at the night sky. I smiled.

Chapter Four

The island quickly became a place of memories. After a few days I became so removed from my former life that whenever I sat down words poured uncensored from my pen. My childhood came to life, and every time I burned something it felt like a new beginning. I left third grade a muddled mess of burned remains, and Cub Scouting was ground into the rocks high above the sea. Climbing trees and eating mulberries were committed to paper and then devoured by flame far more easily than I expected.

I found new places to write each day as I walked. A rock with a view was perfect for my second endeavor and some soft flowers made room for the third. When I wasn't near the water I spread the ashes over the grass or ground them into the rocks and pebbles with my foot. Once in a while, I would find a word or two left unconsumed, floating around the low hills and the high stones. There were a few spots where I wrote so often that the ground began to turn grey with ash.

At first the physical remnants bothered me. I didn't like the idea that my words were not completely gone, and that a child might show up at home having pieced together nearly a full sentence. "Mommy, what does this mean?" the child would cry, holding out a string of words, charred on all sides, and barely comprehensible even in its entirety: *"I pinch my tongue against the roof of my..."* or *"his one blue eye keeps me awake for..."*

But in the end, it was just a fragment. It was never a full thought or a story. Someone might find a sentence at the most, but then I'd be a mystery rather than a failure. I could leave clues without real fear of repercussions, and if my neighbors on the island thought I was a little crazy, then that was okay too.

I sat at the café one morning sipping my coffee and letting thoughts spill through my mind. I had been writing for five days. I wrote about school and work and college, and even Mike and Suzanne crept into my pages. I wrote and I wrote, but as I burned through my first notebook, I felt nothing. It was like burning a paper towel or a newspaper I'd never read. I was starting a fire with kindling that had no other use.

I looked around the café for inspiration, but it was a normal quiet morning in a normal quiet town. Abigail was inside rolling silverware, and the one waiter on shift was smoking by the stone wall looking out over the sea. There was a small window on the second floor of the café with a curtain in bright blue gingham, and I wondered briefly whether someone lived there.

I took a few deep breaths, remembered to forget about what I was doing, and touched my pen to the page.

It's the first week of college and I'm still in love with my high school girlfriend. What makes it worse is that she's a year younger than me and I can't tell anyone. I'm embarrassed and in love, and it's a horrible combination.

I have a job every Saturday morning that requires me to sit at a desk and answer a phone that never rings. I write her letters every week for three months and they get more explicit and depraved as the weeks go by. In one letter all I do is describe what I'll do to her when she comes to visit me. I don't hold back and I tell her everything in as much detail as I can manage. I use words I can't say out loud and by the time I'm finished I'm hard and afraid. It takes me two days to mail it.

Her mother writes back to me instead. She opened the letter without thinking and she was horrified by the contents. She read it over and over again and she got angrier each time. She tells me I'm a terrible influence and a very bad boy. She is going to have to come straighten me out herself.

Her letter smells of perfume.

I closed my notebook and pulled out the Zippo. I flicked it on and off, snapping the lid shut with a satisfying click, but the café patio was not a place to burn pages. I stuffed the notebook back into my bag and waved at the waiter who had just finished his smoking.

"Could I have another cup of coffee?"

"Sure, man. What are you writing?"

"Just journaling," I said.

He nodded and disappeared inside with my cup. I tried to hide my annoyance with the question, but something was nagging me. I was journaling, in a way, but it sounded trite and silly. It sounded like something teenagers do rather than authors. But then again, authors actually write, I thought.

I returned to the house after an hour and two more cups of coffee, stopping along the way to burn my pages by the water. I remembered being scared for a week that my girlfriend's mother had been serious. I watched the page burn and I wondered what had happened to her.

I shook my head as I walked in the font door to find Issa sitting at the piano.

"Hey, James. How was your walk?"

I put my notebook down on the kitchen table and

walked back into the living room.

"It was awesome. I can't believe that you get to live out here all the time. The whole island is so beautiful and the people are so damn friendly. And I love that café."

"Abigail is a genius. I don't know what we'd do without her."

She got up off the piano bench and motioned me over with a hand.

"Do you play?"

I shook my head as I sat down on the couch. Music was not my forte. I played the trumpet for exactly two months when I was in third grade and the guitar for about as long in high school. I had dreams of being in a band that lasted until my fingers started to blister from the strings on my borrowed electric. If I was in a band I would be the guy standing on the side of the stage with a fresh beer and extra guitar strings.

"How's your morning going?" I asked.

Issa sat down on the couch next to me and pulled her knees up under her chin. She was ten years older than me, I'd learned, and at least six times more limber.

"I've been better," she said. "But that's the way it goes, right? Up and down, rain and dry and all that. Sometimes I'm not sure if living out here is a blessing or a curse. I love how pretty it is and I do like the quiet, but my God does it make some things more difficult."

"I used to think that living in New York was hard. It's expensive and busy and it's nearly impossible to be alone. It's noisy all the time, and it's usually too hot or too cold. But maybe everywhere is hard."

She nodded her head and smiled at me. I couldn't picture her living anywhere else, though I assumed she had another life before this one. Before I could ask, she grabbed me by the arm and dragged me over to the piano.

"Let's learn you a few scales. There's nothing better for focusing the mind than playing music, and even if you don't get really good at it, I think you'll like it."

As she showed me where to put my fingers, I tried to focus on the piano rather then her body next to me on the bench. She smelled like jasmine, coffee, and clay, and I hadn't been that close to a woman in a long time. She laughed at me as I tried to play a simple scale, but her patience far outlasted mine. When I finally gave up after nearly an hour she promised me I had done well. I sprawled out on the couch making a scrunched-up face of disappointment.

"I'm terrible at this."

"Well, I would say you haven't done too badly." She flopped down in the big chair across from me and put her feet up on the coffee table.

"I should probably stick to writing," I said.

"How's the book coming along?"

"Eh," I said eloquently. "I'm writing again, which is the important thing, but I'm not really sure it's going anywhere. I suppose it's more of an exercise than anything. Right now I'm feeling mostly useless."

"What's it feel like to burn it? I think I would get sad every time." I had finally told Issa and Paul what I was doing, expecting the same wry smiles and sarcastic comments that I got from my friends back home. I tensed up as I struggled to figure out how to explain myself, but there was no need at all. Paul thought it sounded as useful as how most people spend their time, and Issa said it was a good lesson in attachment.

"It's liberating in a way. I don't have to worry about what I say or how I write. I don't need to be careful about names or histories. I can write anything I like, but I'm still not sure if it's enough."

"It sounds ideal, James," she said. "I've been thinking about making pots that don't work, just to see what it feels like. It's art for art's sake."

"Are you making fun of me?" I asked, trying to sound lighthearted.

"Nope, it's purely out of solidarity. And curiosity. I want to know what it's like. I think I might make a vase out of porous clay that won't hold water. That's going to be my first one. Then I may move on to a teapot with no spout. I feel like it may drive me a bit crazy, but I think it will be good for me. I'm way too practical sometimes."

"You're the first person to take this even slightly seriously. At home I think most of my friends were humoring me. Or blatantly insulting me. But it's complicated."

"I think it's a cool idea. Besides, it sounds almost spiritual to me. You're writing something, then burning it as an offering."

"It's not an offering any god would want, that's for sure."

"Well, either way, I'm glad you're here. It's been nice having someone around during the day, even if we're off doing our own things."

We sat for a while before she got up and made her way back to her studio. I couldn't help myself from turning around and watching her ass as she walked down the hall. Right before she closed the door, she turned to me and winked.

That evening I wrote down by the water once more. It was nearly impossible to do, but maybe that was part of what I liked about it. I had to wedge myself into a seat that was not especially comfortable, and I squinted just so I could see my page. On occasion I held a flashlight between my teeth, but it always left me tempted to reread things.

One day a professor of mine tells me to stay away from fiction. She means it as a compliment, but all I hear is that I lack imagination. She's twenty years older than me and every guy in my class wants to sleep with her. I love her and hate her, and I get myself off thinking about her dragging me into her office to give me private lessons.

For two months I write about her nonstop. When I write she's either in my bed or against the blackboard in the lecture hall. I write down every little detail, describing the way she stands and how she holds the chalk. I write about her voice and her shoes, and my fantasies never end.

There is no fiction in what I want.

The page took forever to catch. I tried six times to get it lit, but the wind was strong and the paper was damp. I didn't want to think about school and I didn't want to remember the notebooks I filled with insane fantasies, but it was all there anyway. I laughed at myself as I remembered, but it was tinged with guilt and possibly a touch of shame.

When the page finally caught I held it out over the rocks until it burned my fingers. It blackened my skin and left a sticky stain that I couldn't rub off. I closed my eyes to the wind and tried to let it all go. The memory was gone, the words were gone, and I was somewhere new. The island could take care of its own.

Chapter Five

Up at the house, Stephen was back in his room and Paul and Issa were sitting on the porch drinking wine, hands intertwined. It was a ritual I was quickly getting used to.

"How's the writing going?" Paul asked when I opened the screen door.

"Very soon I'll have burned an entire novel. I can sell it in an empty box and let the reader discover it on their own. That would work, right? I mean, you'd buy an invisible book, wouldn't you?"

"Oh, definitely," Issa said. "Right, Paul? We'd read it in bed together as we listened to the sound of the waves and we'd tell each other how romantic it was."

Issa leaned her head on Paul's shoulder and for a moment I remembered her sitting next to me on the piano bench. I felt a twinge of guilt and regret.

"So what's the deal, James?" Paul asked. "I understand the experiment, but from what Stephanie says, you're good at this. Not to pry, but what's going on? This would be a good place to actually write a book."

"Do you mind?" I asked as I reached down to the open bottle of wine.

"Let me get more," he said as he stood up and walked into the house.

Issa leaned in and whispered,

"He drank the first bottle on his own. Don't mind him. He means well."

A minute later Paul returned with another glass and a new bottle of Pinot noir, this time from California. He uncorked it, and poured me some. Then he poured one for Issa and one for himself. When he finally leaned back into the couch he looked over at me with a calm smile. Paul was too patient for comfort.

"The short story is that my last novel led to an ugly breakup that left me a bit of a mess. It sounds ridiculous when I say it out loud, but that's my story and I'm sticking to it. Writing for me has always been a way for me to understand the people around me. I wrote notes to girls in class when I couldn't talk to them, and all through school I found myself able to put things down on paper that I couldn't say with words. I wrote letters long after people stopped writing letters, and I thought it was the only thing I was good at. It let me know people I wouldn't otherwise know.

"And then I realized that it could go both ways. I knew I could make people happy or excited by things I wrote, but with Jane I realized I could do other things as well. I wrote something terrible and..."

"You don't have to explain everything," Issa said. "I think we all know what breakups can be like."

Paul nodded, and I took the opportunity to sip my wine and stare out over the water. It was my turn to break the silence.

"How long have you been married?"

"Six years."

"Five years," Paul corrected her. "We've been married for five years, but we met six years ago. It was a brief engagement followed by an even briefer wedding."

"We got married out here on the island, and only some of my family came out. They weren't super excited that I was moving all the way across the country to marry a man I'd just met. Heaven forbid they have to come visit if they want to see me. I mean, I know it's not the prettiest place in the world, but..."

Issa trailed off into her wine glass.

"Is Stephen okay that I'm here?"

"He's used to us having visitors. I think he likes the company as well. He's mostly stuck with his parents. Trust me. He'll let you know if he's unhappy." Even when he was being snarky Paul didn't sound unkind.

"I'm not used to being around kids."

"Yeah, and don't call him a kid either," Issa added. "But since he's not here right now, maybe it's a good time for us to bring something up. Paul?"

He looked at his wife, then back at me. Then back at Issa. I could see him thinking as I sat there patiently, but it was Issa who finally continued.

"Paul and I have an open marriage. It's not too crazy or anything, but we both have some long-term partners who we see occasionally. Well, at least Paul does. I just got out of something a few weeks ago, and I'm still struggling with it."

I took a much bigger sip of my wine than I might have, and maybe I shouldn't confess that the first thing I thought of was Issa and me on the couch that afternoon. Open marriages might mean a whole bunch of things, and I was suddenly looking at her with new eyes.

"Has it always been that way? I mean, did you get married knowing it was going to be open?"

"It's her fault."

Issa kicked him under the table and crossed her arms over her chest.

"Yes, I forced you to go out and sleep with other women. You poor husband. How ever did you survive?"

"Okay, maybe it's not so bad." Paul was grinning from ear to ear. "But it was her idea. Or at least her requirement. That's not right either. The point is that when she accepted my invitation to move out here it was something that was important to her. What did you say, darling? I'm not the type of person who gets my needs met in one place. Talk about the driest way of saying you like to get some on the side."

"Don't be a dick, Paul. We've both been married before, and while we love each other, and love living out here in the middle of nowhere, we don't believe that fidelity and commitment require exclusivity."

"Hey, I'm not one to judge your marriage," I protested. "I can barely manage one relationship at a time, but that's my problem. It sounds like it's working for you."

"It's working better for him right now. My girlfriend decided that she wanted to give monogamy a try, blah blah blah." She was smiling, but there was a hint of sadness in her eyes. I realized it had been there since I arrived, and now it made sense.

"Does Stephen know?" I asked.

"He does," Issa said. "It was probably the most awkward conversation we've ever had, but he got used to it fairly quickly. He doesn't want to know too much, which is fine with us, but we feel it's important to keep him in the loop. Especially when it affects our life out here. He's a part of the family and has a right to be involved in decisions that impact him."

"Anyway, James, the reason we're telling you this is that Stephen and I are going to spend a night on the mainland with my partner Mariko. She has a son Stephen's age, and I have a conference on the mainland that goes late tomorrow anyway. So, we're going to spend the night out there at her place. We didn't want it to be weird, or for you to wonder what was going on."

"Paul's worried about being a creep. He's afraid you'll see him flirting with the waitress at the café and think he's a horrible husband to me. Which is totally true, but for different reasons."

"I'm a perfect husband and you know it."

"Yes dear."

My head was spinning from more than the wine, but I didn't know what to say at all. My first thought—after Issa and the piano—was about me and Jane. I slipped into wondering what our life would have been like if we dated other people. Would it have made things easier or more difficult? Would it have let us salvage anything at all?

After a moment I realized they were waiting for me to say something. "Well, Stephanie did say you two were 'like totally open and shit.' Now it all makes sense."

"My niece has such a way with words. I'm so glad she warned you."

I stood up more abruptly than I had intended, but the wine and the thinking were doing me no good.

"Well, I think I've had enough wine, and my back is sore from sitting down on the rocks all night. I'm going to get some sleep. See you both in the morning?"

"You can always take a chair down with you. Or at least a pillow," Issa said as I walked past her and into the house.

"Sleep tight," Paul called from the porch.

I walked down the hallway to my room and closed the door behind me. It was stuffy and warm, so I opened the window to the cool breeze coming in off the sea. I changed into my pajamas, climbed into bed, and picked up the postcard that Suzanne had thoughtfully addressed to herself. I turned it over and stared at the picture. I picked up my pen and tried to think of something to say, but nothing sounded good at all. I turned out the light, put the postcard back down on the table, closed my eyes, and slept.

Chapter Six

The next morning Stephen mentioned Sebastien at breakfast.

"Who's that again? I can never keep track of your friends," Paul asked.

"He's not my friend," Stephen said irritably. "He's renting the room over Abigail's. You must have seen him."

"Maybe we should invite him for dinner," Issa mumbled between sips of coffee. "Is he French? It might be nice to have a Frenchman over for dinner. Is he handsome?"

"For an old guy. But he also speaks six or seven languages. Abigail says that he reads papers in Italian, but his English is perfect. He's here for a few weeks, but he's totally the coolest person that's ever come out here."

"Well, if Issa and James see him at the café they can invite him out. I'm always happy to welcome a new visitor to the island. Even if he is French."

"Dad, I want to invite him. I saw him first."

"What is he, a puppy, Stephen?"

"Come on, we're going to be late. And probably miss him anyway."

The two of them gathered their things and made their way out the door as Issa and I stood up to say goodbye. It was a cold morning, but it looked like sun for the rest of the day.

"Okay, kids. We're staying on the mainland tonight so you'll have to fend for yourselves. Don't drink any of the good wine, and don't forget to eat supper."

"Thanks, Dad!" Issa said with a grin before giving him a hug and a kiss that were clearly more sincere. "I'll miss you."

"I'll miss you too." And with that, they were off.

We hadn't left the breakfast table, other than to say goodbye, and I was still in my shorts and t-shirt. My mug had gone cold in my hand, but neither one of us seemed inclined to move.

"Does it bother you when he goes off with someone else? I don't know if I could deal with it. My ex-girlfriend started dating someone three months after we broke up, and even that was enough to drive me crazy. I can't imagine just sending her off like that."

"It helps that I know he'll come home. I mean, it is his house and all. But it's definitely gotten easier. I think it's safe to say the first few times I was not all calm and zen about it. In fact, I believe there was gnashing of teeth and a few sleepless nights."

"You're a better woman than I am."

"You're not wrong about that. Now you go do your writer thing while I go do my potter thing, and tonight we can open the good wine and get drunk on the porch."

"Like we do every night."

"Exactly."

After cleaning up from breakfast, I took Issa's advice and grabbed a pillow off the couch before making my way back down to the water. The waves were crashing softly against the rocks and they called to me. I looked about until I found the nook in the rocks, and I squished my pillow down into the crevice until I was comfortable. Okay, James. You're going to fucking write something, and it's not going to be about the cute redhead inside who is elbow deep in wet clay.

I looked down at my notebook, hoping a story would come, but despite my best efforts all I could think of was Jane.

The first time I kiss Jane is at a rooftop party. We have all the same friends, and none of the same circles. Somehow we float by each other's lives like jetsam without ever succumbing to the other's gravity.

The sun is going down and the roof is hot and full of sweaty people drinking beer from cans. Jane is leaning against the railing in tight blue jeans and a tank top from CBGB's. Her hair is short and cropped tightly around her ears, and she's smoking a Lucky Strike like an old man.

"Filters are too slow?" I ask.

"If you're going to do something, I say go all the way."

"Well, I'm a second-hand smoker, but I appreciate the philosophy."

"To each their own. You're James, right? I see you at all these things, but somehow we never actually talk."

"Yeah, I'm intimidated by you. It's the shirt, and the hair, and the grandpa cigarettes."

"They do have that effect. It's too bad though, I think you're cute."

I lean in closer to her and inhale the smoke as it leaves her mouth. She doesn't move away, and when she looks right at me it's a challenge. I take another step and she puts a hand on my waist as she takes another long drag off her cigarette.

"I also love the way smokers taste," I whisper.

She drops her butt to the black tar roof and our mouths find each other instantly. We don't stop until long after the sun goes down.

I burned the page without reading it. Memories are supposed to be left alone, especially when they're about Jane. They fade over time for a reason, and if we hold on too tightly we pine for something other than what is. It's not healthy and it's far too easy to get lost. Memories tell us nothing.

The afternoon was peaceful. Issa and I spent hours preparing a meal for ourselves. The night finally brought relief from the heat of the afternoon sun, and we opened the windows to let in the cool breeze. We shared a bottle of Cabernet as we cooked and another with dinner so that by the time we were finished eating, the room was tipsy and the wind was definitely drunk. I sat on the piano bench making awful sounds that Issa laughed and cringed at. Finally I fell down onto the couch leaving the keys to their own endeavors. All the windows were open and the breeze blew in as we sat and talked. She told me her story for the first time, and I gave my best impression of a good listener.

"Paul and I met six years ago. It either feels like twice as long or half. Depending on the day I suppose. I was doing consulting work in Boston after my divorce, and my God the work was so awful. It paid amazingly well and I honestly didn't know what else to do with myself. I was suddenly single and had far too much time on my hands. But it was terrible, James. What the hell was I thinking?" She laughed as she spoke, but there was a seriousness in her voice.

"I was good at it, and they kept promoting me and telling me I was brilliant, but who cares? Only my direct supervisor understood just how miserable I was and in some ways that made it worse. He used to take me out for lunch and ask me over and over again if I was happy there. I smiled and nodded, and every once in a while I threw my hands up and told him I didn't know what else to do.

"And then I met Paul. He was at a conference in Boston. He was handsome and kind, and he lacked the stress and anxiety of everyone I worked with. He was there to figure out how to promote his wine company, and I was there doing my stupid job. We talked during a terrible presentation and we didn't stop until we had finished dinner, three drinks, and a kiss. He invited me out to the island the next day, and I just said fuck it. There was nothing keeping me there but ambition I resented and a paycheck I was tired of craving. When I stepped off the ferry I felt like I was home, James. There's no other way to describe it. I walked off the boat, I looked Paul in the eyes, and told him I didn't ever want to leave.

"The next day I called my supervisor and told him I was done. He actually laughed at me and told me it was about time.

He covered my ass at work and within a week it all felt so far away I could hardly remember it had actually been my life. Stephen was warm and energetic, and he was excited I was here. I was terrified he would hate me and resent me, but we talked and talked the first three nights until morning, and within a week I had a new best friend who was seven years old. I was home, and it was perfect."

"For six months I didn't leave the island, and my entire family came up to see if I had gone crazy. Paul was amazing throughout it all. He welcomed them into our home, poured them endless glasses of wine, and gave them the grand tour. They still thought I was nuts, but I was so happy even they had to see it. They watched me cook and work with my hands, and they didn't know what to say. I was so clearly in love with Paul, Stephen, and the island that in the end they didn't even try to drag me away.

"It was my friend Gray on the other side of the island who showed up one day with a potter's wheel. It was old and had belonged to her grandmother, but she helped me get it working and taught me how to throw pots. I don't know what possessed her, but when she walked through the door the first time she said, 'Girl, you need to work with those hands.'

"And I did. I threw pots obsessively for weeks and Paul said he felt like I already had a new boyfriend with that wheel. When we got married, workers just showed up one morning to build a kiln. It was my wedding present from Paul, and I cried and I cried until I couldn't stand it. We got married here at the house, and the entire island showed up to celebrate with us. They felt like family after just one year, and I had never felt anything like that before. I never had a tight group of friends, let alone a family of my choosing. I never thought life could be like this at all, and it was amazing until…"

"Until what?" I asked. I had been patient, but I was hanging on every word. I wanted to know everything there was to know about her, and this felt important. She leaned back in her chair and took a drink before shaking her head like she was coming out of a trance.

"It's still amazing. Sometimes I just wonder if I would have been content doing it like everyone else does."

"The whole open thing?" I asked with a hint of curiosity in my voice that I couldn't hide. She looked down for a moment, as if she wasn't sure how to answer, but she never stopped smiling. She nodded her head as she took her time answering me.

"Marriage is always an adventure, and when you decide to include other people it's even more so. But after my first marriage, there was no way I could do monogamy again. I love Paul, and we work well together, but neither one of us likes the idea of ownership. Plus learning to live here, having a teenager in the house, and everything else, comes with its own troubles and concerns." Her voice trailed off, and while I was still full of questions I kept my mouth shut. I had learned more about her in an hour than in the previous week, and I didn't want to do a thing to ruin the friendship we were slowly building.

She was so close to me on the couch that I could feel her body's warmth, and every time I turned she was smiling at me with an invitation to something I didn't understand. I leaned back and she did the same. When my hand brushed her leg, she didn't move it, and when our feet rubbed together neither one of us said a thing. I felt her head lean down onto my shoulder, and I had to hold my breath; it took everything I had not to kiss her.

But when I touched her hair the spell was broken. I pushed my fingers through her curls, and instead of leaning closer against me, she sat up to take another sip of her wine. I stretched my arms above my head, yawned, and stood up. We had gotten way too close for comfort, and if I sat there a minute longer I was going to do something I couldn't take back.

Outside the sun had gone down, and the two empty wine bottles on the kitchen table reminded me of where I was. The breeze was cool and Issa looked so comfortable that I wanted to stay there forever. She was brilliant and beautiful, but she was also so many things I didn't understand. What would Paul think if he saw us sitting here? Was kissing allowed, or did I have to ask someone permission? If I couldn't bring myself to even ask the question, then I had no business doing anything else. I shook my head and got myself a glass of water.

"I think I'm going to write some more."

She looked up at me with wide eyes, and I wasn't sure what was there. She smiled and nodded, but she was silent. I tried to push into her mind, if only to see a glimpse of what she was thinking, but there was nothing. I turned, and walked down the hall on shaky feet without saying another word.

I didn't go too far from the house, but I found a spot amid the white rocks and scraggly vegetation where I nestled down. The writing again came easily with my hand greased by the wine and my mind perfectly willing to write without thought, judgment, or doubt. My high from talking with Issa hadn't faded at all, and I allowed myself to follow images without concern for censor. Music began to have flavor and I could taste the expressions of passers-by in the street. I slid down roads rather than walked, and the buildings and rivers surrounding me drifted off into misty memories and bright arcades. I filled a page with only four words and let it burn. Time moved in circles through lives and deaths without regard for before or after.

Red hair, green eyes, strong hands, windblown laughs that keep me up at night. If I was a real writer I would have kissed her and she would have smiled and it would be a story I'd write over and over again. I'd write her head onto my pillow and she'd laugh at me and with me until the gulls woke us up in the morning.

If I was a real writer.

I burned it, hoping to make it true, and out of nowhere more memories began to appear. My mind found itself wandering the streets of New York, and as always, there was Jane.

Jane is going to meet me for coffee. One kiss on a roof and it's coffee downtown with no promises of anything. I change my shirt three times because I know that I'm not cool enough for her, and we end up wearing the same thing. Her jeans are tighter and her shirt is blacker, but our boots are nearly identical and she laughs with me when the waiter asks if we're in a band.

Later that night we kiss again. It starts out slowly, but this time it doesn't stop. We move from the coffee shop to the street and then someone's stoop in the East Village. I pull her onto my lap and she scratches my chest through my shirt.

"Will you think I'm a whore if I fuck you on our first date?" she asks.

I didn't even watch it burn. It was gone and it was best forgotten. I turned to the next page and kept on going.

I'm not sure how long I sat there swaying and writing and trying not to think. I read a few of the pages over again before I burned them, and others I just sent from my pen to a match without so much as a glance. I took breaks and stared up at the stars, and remembered home with a fondness I hadn't felt in over a year. I sat there, holding onto it, and I felt completely alive.

After hours of writing, my back began to feel the pressure of the rocks, and my mind was tired and nearly sober. I pulled myself up and spread the ashes around with my foot before walking back to the house.

My room was cool as I changed into pajamas. The bathroom was dark as I washed my face, and the rest of the house was silent but for the sound of creaking wood and wind. Stephen's door was open, making it obvious that he wasn't home, and no sound came from Paul and Issa's room. Even the studio was dark, and the only light in the house came from the night sky as it splashed the floors and walls through the windows and curtains. I finally slipped into my room, pulled back the blankets, and climbed into bed and the comfort of exhausted sleep.

A soft chord woke me at an indeterminable hour of the night, and I lay there and listened to make sure I was awake. More notes drifted by my room. I felt hot with the door closed, so I got out of bed and made my way to the hall. I opened the door with one hand, and leaned the other against the wall as the music got louder. I walked out and turned the corner. I could hear the softness of her fingers on the piano keys trying not to make too much noise. The windows were still open and the wind was blowing through the grasses and the trees outside. The music flowed quietly through the house, and the smell of our dinner lingered in the air as it was carried down to the rocky shore.

I looked around the corner, afraid of the image I might happen upon and what I might do. My mind was still full of every lurid detail I had written, and Issa's face had come to mind more than once. The crimson red of her hair covered the near side of her face as she played. She was wearing a simple cotton shirt, unbuttoned at the front, and rolled at the sleeves. The far side of her shirt had fallen off her shoulder and the curve of her left breast was barely visible in the moonlight. Another bottle of wine sat atop the piano with a half-empty glass next to it. As she played, her head moved with her hands and her lips opened just enough to give her breath.

The warmth of the day still lingered, and even as I felt the cool wetness of a damp shirt against my back, an enviable bead of sweat slid slowly down her neck and between her breasts until it was lost in shadows still hidden by moonlight. As her hands continued to move over the polished keys, she arched her shoulders just enough to slide the shirt down her back. One at a time, her arms left the sleeves. I could see her breasts in the dim light, and I ached to be closer as much as I feared it. Her silhouette beckoned me until I closed my eyes to keep from moving.

I leaned against the wall with my eyes closed, allowing the music to cloud my senses more than her skin already had. The notes lapped effortlessly at the walls and the wind hummed through the open windows as I tried to imagine the traffic of New York and found that I couldn't. When I finally opened my eyes I noticed that the music had faded away, and Issa's hands had moved to her stomach in a circular motion. Her fingers wiped away sweat, and her head leaned forward to rest against the piano. I heard her lips open with a breath as her left hand slid between her thighs, and she swayed slowly with the wind.

The moonlight flickered across her body with the movement of curtains, and she sat there with her toes gripping the cool copper of a pedal. Her lips let in more breath as her hand moved faster, and she brushed the hair out of her eyes until it sprawled on her freckled shoulders. I turned quietly and leaned against the wall as I tried to distinguish her soft moans from the summer breeze, and as I began to walk back to my room I heard her moans increase to a final sigh of release. When I reached my door I heard the music begin once again, even slower this time, and the soft sound of the hammers on the strings echoed through the house and night air.

I left my door open as I climbed back into bed, and I remember waking briefly to the shadow of a woman passing my door with a white shirt dragging softly behind her.

Chapter Seven

The smell of coffee and the sounds in the kitchen woke me late in the morning. Sleep had left only a few images in my head that disappeared when I opened my eyes. I took my backpack with me as I walked down the hall. Issa was in a light cotton robe, cooking an omelette.

"Hey James, did you sleep well?" she asked with a yawn.

I nodded as I slipped down into the depths of the oversized chair. "How about you?"

"I needed that," she answered as she sat down on the piano bench with her breakfast. "After you went off last night I got so inspired. I sat for hours at the wheel throwing pots until I couldn't hold my head up. The smell got stronger with each pot. It was wonderful."

"I think there must have been something in the air. I finished an entire notebook in one sitting." I slouched down in between the thick pillows and caught myself staring at her toes as they tapped on the polished brass foot pedal. She continued to talk about her work, and my eyes continued wandering from the open windows back to the boxers and small tank top she was wearing. It fit loosely over her strong shoulders and small breasts, and I started to count her freckles until she said my name.

"James? Are you okay? You look out of it."

I sat up, startled and embarrassed.

"I was just dozing off. I'm still sleepy and I can't seem to keep my mind on any one thing. And also, you look super hot." I'm sure I was blushing, but the words slipped out before I could stop them.

"You know, I'm beginning to think Paul made a good choice when he invited you up here. I wasn't sure at first, but I think I like you."

"Well, I'll have to thank him when he gets home."

"You should. He'll appreciate it. But listen, my friend Gray is going to take some of my pots to the mainland this afternoon. Do you want to go into town with me after you eat?"

A visit to the café and a talk with Abigail sounded like just what the doctor ordered. After I scrounged breakfast and cleaned up, we headed outside to where her bike was leaning against the house. She had two pots with her that looked like they had just been fired, and she placed them in the basket in front of the handlebars. It was at that point that I remembered that we only had one bike for the two of us, and when she climbed on and patted the basket in the back I must have let out a whimper.

"Oh come on, Stephen and I do this all the time," she said. "Just be sure to hold on. But don't squeeze too tightly," she added. I finally straddled the back of the bike, wrapped my arms around Issa's waist and as we started to roll down the path I was blown away by a burst of fiery red hair lapping at my face in the wind. I felt silly and alive, and there was nowhere else I wanted to be.

It usually takes about ten minutes to get into town with just one person on the bike, but with the two of us bumbling along on the rocky path, it took us almost twenty before we entered the small cluster of houses and shops. Issa dropped me off at the post office, which also served as a small store for household items, beer, and maple syrup. I picked up a new notebook and said a few words of hello to the man behind the counter before heading out the door towards the café.

The street in town ran along the south side of the small bay, and it was quiet and peaceful in the early afternoon. The bay was the only place on the island one could even think of landing a boat, so naturally the village had sprung up there. The town was more a scattering of houses and a few small shops than anything else, but there were always people out and about lackadaisically fighting entropy. A woman across the street was busy painting the walls of a small stone patio, and down the way an old man was planting flowers along a walkway. A few children played in the street, chasing after each other and then collapsing in the heat of the afternoon. They all smiled and said hi as I walked by, every one of them knowing I was a New York writer with a fetish for dark coffee.

It was a short walk to the café, and as I approached it I saw Abigail sitting outside on the patio wall staring out over the water. The café was a small two-story building, whitewashed and sea sanded, and again I found myself looking up at the second floor to where, according to Stephen, Sebastien was staying. Two windows looked out over the street, and both of them were open allowing the brightly colored curtains to blow freely in the breeze. There was a metal balcony under one of the windows and for some strange reason it brought back memories of New Orleans.

"Abigail!" I cried as I walked up from the street. "How the hell are you?"

"New York!" she answered me. "I'm not bad at all. Just watching the boys pull up some pots from the harbor. We'll have fresh lobster on the menu tonight. Why are you so late?"

"I had things to do this morning. Besides, it's never too late for a good cup of coffee."

Every time someone passed by on the street Abigail would call out to them by name, wishing them a good day and asking

about a member of their family who was having some diffi-
culty. I sat and listened to their conversations while I looked out
over the bay in search of the lobstermen she mentioned. When
I finally moved to my table, Abigail brought out two cups of
coffee and sat with me. The winter had been good for fishing,
she said, and the warm weather was good for her business.

"So, have you met Sebastien yet?" she asked.

"Nope. Never heard of him."

"He's renting my spare room. He says he came from Italy,
but he's clearly French. Not that I was snooping, but I like
people who say what they are. Who comes to Maine from Italy?
Anyway, I have no use for the room. I'm sure you'll meet him
if you stay long enough. He also likes to sit and do nothing but
drink wine and watch boats. You foreigners are all the same."
She laughed warmly as she spoke, and I wondered how long she
had lived here. For all I knew Abigail was born on the island and
had never left.

"Abigail, I'm from New York. It's not a foreign country."

"It might as well be," she said wistfully. Then more quietly,
"So tell me, can you still buy pot in Washington Square Park?"

"Abigail!" I said in mock surprise.

"Listen, New York, just because I look like an old lady to
you doesn't mean I wasn't young once."

It had never occurred to me to refer to her as an old lady,
and even as she said it, it seemed as absurd as calling the wind
old. Abigail was just Abigail.

"You can't buy anything you'd want to smoke. Besides,
everyone delivers now. You call them up and before you know it
they're at your door with more choices than you know what to
do with. It's a strange new world."

"Well, that doesn't sound as much fun. Easy though," she
added before jumping up and walking over to where one of her
kids was struggling to correctly set a table.

I sat quietly drinking my coffee. When I caught myself fiddling with the straps of my bag, I finally brought out the new notebook and began to write.

The first time Jane spends the night we can't sleep.

It's hot and my air conditioner is broken. We assume that enough gin and a cold shower will leave us in such a state of frenzy that we'll fuck until we pass out. In the end there is no fucking. There is far too much gin, but there is nothing close to passing out.

Jane gets up three times in the night to lurch over the toilet and empty her stomach, while I soak towels in cold water and cover my head in hopes that it might cool me down. When I'm good I hold her hair away from her face, and when she doesn't slam the door behind her I sit and tell her everything will be okay.

When we finally leave my apartment the next day she's pale as a ghost. We eat breakfast at the Waverly Diner but even eggs and bacon don't do much for her color.

"On the bright side, if we can survive that night, I bet we can live through anything," she says.

"Did we survive the night? I assumed you never wanted to see me again."

"Well, you did hold my hair a few times. I'll give you another shot."

And right then, hungover and exhausted, I have my first glimmer of hope.

The weight of the pages became noticeable after an hour, and I tore them from the book and snuck into the kitchen of the café. Abigail had grown used to my eccentricities and generally looked the other way. I tossed the bundle of pages into the small wood stove and walked back through the kitchen to my table, where I took a sip of my now cold coffee and poured out more words. New York was gone and I was back on a different island surrounded by different people. I breathed in the fresh air and looked out over the water.

When I eventually looked back at the café, I noticed a man sitting on the far side of the patio reading a paper and smoking a hand-rolled cigarette. He had a handsome face with strong features, and I could gather nothing in his expressions but a faint interest in the words he was reading. He smiled and cocked his head when he noticed me staring at him, and I waved back offering a brief hello. He had a glass of wine sitting in front of him, and one foot rested on the opposite knee as he leaned back in his chair. He was poised and well-dressed.

Just then Issa pulled up on the bike and waved at me to hop on. "Hi Sebastien!" she shouted from the street, and he waved at her with a friendly smile and another nod. I gathered up my things and climbed onto the back of the bicycle. I nearly dropped my backpack as I tried to settle myself, and it took a moment before I was properly seated on the back of the bike. I felt like a child.

"Hello, Melissa," he called back and she stopped so short that I almost fell off.

"I know why I know who you are, but why do you know who I am?" she asked.

"It's easy," he replied. "I have been told the prettiest woman on island is called Melissa. It must be you."

I could have heard her blush, but she didn't say a word. She waved again before pushing the bike along with a strong kick. As we started off, I couldn't help feel incredibly foolish with my arms wrapped around her waist as a strange man watched us go down the street with his dark eyes and steady gaze. I could still smell the cigarette he had been smoking.

"How did you know that was Sebastien?" I asked in her ear, my chin resting on her shoulder.

"He's the only person on the island I've never seen before. Who else could it be?"

The ride home was exhilarating, and the heat of the sun

left beads of sweat dripping down our faces as we maneuvered along the path. I still had images in my head, and words ready to come, but the pressure to write that I had felt for the last few days was gone. There would be time to write, time to stare at pages, and all that mattered now was the wind, the sun, and the pressure of Issa's body against mine as we pulled up to the house.

We ate a late lunch after the painting was finished and it felt good to be home. Issa was feeling better than she had in the morning and my memory of her playing the piano was beginning to blur and blend into fragments of words on charred paper. My recollection of the entire evening was so messy that by the time the sun began to lower in the sky I couldn't remember if I had stopped writing before or after Issa woke me with her soft fingers and humming strings.

Chapter Eight

I was on fire. I finished a page and held it out over the candle. Page two now. Where was I? I couldn't remember, and it didn't matter. I was a master, a poet, and a fucking novelist. I could make worlds and destroy them and no one could stop me, because the words were mine as soon as they burned. I could write love, sex, and death, and they all belonged to me in a way they never had before. I could touch and taste and there was no reason to think as I let my emotions pour out onto the page. I was the master and there was no one there to tell me what I did or didn't understand.

Jane paints with her hair on fire. Her body sways in the evening sun and she shines so brightly I can't look at her. She takes blank canvas and turns it into things I can't imagine, and her strokes are stronger than any words I can write.

One morning I wake up to her painting me. She's standing naked by the window and I'm hard beneath the sheets. I try not to open my eyes but I can't resist the temptation. Soon my hand finds its way beneath the blanket until it's wrapped around my cock, and she never stops. She paints faster as I move, and when I finally come she's laughing.

The painting hangs above our bed for two years. It's a reminder that some mornings are better than others.

I read it twice before holding it beneath the lighter. As it started to burn I had one brief moment where I wanted desperately to put it out. I wanted to read it again, if only to remember, and I wanted to take it somewhere else. I had burned more fragments than I could remember, but these words felt real to me. After all these years, it was possible that my college writing professor was right.

With everything running around in my head I made my way back up to the house. It was nearly time for dinner, and Stephen and Paul would be home. Again I tried to picture Jane kissing me goodbye to go spend the night with another man, and I laughed when I saw my own face.

"Hey James!" called Stephen as I approached the back door. Paul was nowhere to be seen, but Issa sat next to Stephen on the couch with an open bottle of Cabernet Franc.

"Hey James," she said as I walked in. She reached out and squeezed my hand as I walked by her to sit down in the empty chair.

"What're we up to, kids?"

"I am so effin' glad to be home," said Stephen. "When I spend too much time—"

"Like one night," interrupted Issa.

"Away from the island," Stephen continued, ignoring her, "I remember why I like it out here. Everyone at the conference was just so boring. Wine this and wine that. It's like they all need an excuse to drink so much of the stuff. And then Mariko's kid Tak was sick, so I was stuck watching movies all night by myself. Like I couldn't have done that at home in my room."

"Well, you didn't miss anything out here," said Issa. "James and I got some painting done, I started throwing some vases, and I imagine James lit some fires down by the water. Oh yeah," she added, winking at me, "we also practiced the piano."

"Well," said Stephen, thankfully oblivious as I turned so red I thought I might burst, "I'm still glad to be home.

I don't know how anyone lives out there. There are far too many people."

"I had a good time writing this evening," I finally said. I wasn't sure if I was trying to convince them or myself, but I was feeling compelled to talk about it, if only to unload my emotional baggage for a while.

"What did you write about?" asked Stephen, obviously glad to talk about something other than the conference.

"I don't know. Mostly about New York and my ex-girlfriend Jane. I wrote about bars and cafés because every time Abigail asks me about something, it ends up in my book. Why is she so obsessed with the city? I never figure out what's going to happen until it does which is why it's so much fun. It's like I get to write a story and read it at the same time."

"Is that how the first book worked?" Issa asked.

I laughed a little when I thought about it.

"Actually, with the first book I wrote a solid outline, and did some serious character development. Maybe that's why it was so terrible."

"I saw some decent reviews online," Stephen said, shocking both of us.

"You read my reviews?" I asked. "Why? When?"

"Hey, we had a writer coming to live with us. I wanted to know if you were famous or something. Sounds like a lot of people liked it."

"Well, not everyone, that's for sure. Sometimes I wonder how anyone writes a damn thing these days. All I know is that if you have friends, don't name your characters after them."

"You can name one after me," Stephen said without pause. I looked at him, and found myself getting emotional. I felt ridiculous, but his simple gesture took me completely by surprise, and made me wonder what it would have been like if all my friends were as smart as this fourteen-year-old kid.

"Maybe I will," I said quietly as I took another sip of wine. I focused on my breath and tried not to get too carried away in thought.

"James, did you invite that Sebastien guy over for dinner?" Stephen asked suddenly.

"I didn't get to talk to him. I saw him sitting at the café, though. Looks like a nice guy."

"Well, sometimes I see him on my way to the boat in the morning. I could ask him tomorrow if you want. I mean, if it's okay."

"Stephen, do you really think a forty-year-old man is going to accept a dinner invitation from a teenager? I mean, it's a little odd."

"Whatever. I just get bored with you two all the time."

"Hey, what about me?"

"Sorry. I get bored with you three all the time."

"Thanks, dude."

"One of us will ask him tomorrow, okay?" Issa said.

"We need more kids on the island. Maybe we can import some. Is that legal?"

I stared at Stephen sitting there on the porch. He looked out of place. He was right; there were far too few children to make the place much fun. He was living in an adult world and he was almost entirely alone.

"I think it's bed time. If you two don't mind, I'm going to go join my husband."

Issa got up and left us sitting there with just one lantern burning.

"It's got to be weird growing up here."

"I don't know," he said with a shrug. "I guess as weird as any place else. I mean, I bet growing up in a big city would be strange too. I like sailing, and I like swimming, but sometimes it's just boring. Where did you grow up?"

I closed my eyes for a moment and realized how little I

wanted to share about my childhood. It was more mundane than anything else, but it brought back too many memories that I didn't want to deal with. Memories I had already burned.

"I grew up in the suburbs. Which is a really strange place to live. It's not quiet and pretty like the country and there's not anything fun to do like in a city. It's constantly stuck in the middle without having its own identity. I loved it."

"You're weird, man. At least you probably had other kids to hang out with."

"Sometimes. I mostly sat in my room, played computer games, and wrote stupid stories."

"Sounds about right to me. And sorry about saying you were boring before. You're definitely more interesting than most people who come visit Dad or Issa. I mean, they have okay friends, the but the whole thing is a little weird, if you know what I mean."

"I can imagine. Well, sort of."

"Yeah. Like I said. Weird. Okay, I'm going to bed too. See you tomorrow. Thanks for staying up and talking."

"You too."

I carried the empty wine glasses into the house after he left and set them down in the sink. Washing could wait until the morning. As I turned back towards the hallway I saw a letter sitting on the counter addressed to me.

It was from Jane.

I carried it back to my room, and turned on the lamp by my bed. It had some weight to it, and I wasn't sure if I wanted to open it at all. New York felt so far away, despite my writing, and while she had just been on my mind, I was finally getting settled into a new life. I opened it anyway, and sat there in my room reading it slowly. Once I finished, I read it over again, and finally a third time. I had no idea what to make of it, least of all how to respond.

Jane had broken up with her boyfriend and needed to get out of the city. She knew it was crazy, she wrote, but was there any way she could come visit for a week?

There are some things that you can't actively figure out. You have to sit with them, or let them evolve on their own, and this was one of those things. There was no way I could force myself to say yes or no, and no way I could make myself understand what I wanted. Jane wanted to come here. She had had a new boyfriend, and it was over, and she needed to get away. She needed to leave New York and come to me.

I wanted to read everything into the letter that I could, but what was the point? Jane was a force of nature, and trying to understand her always left me feeling foolish. Her words were clear, however, and they required a response. They demanded an answer.

I eventually shoved the letter into the drawer in my bedside table next to the one I'd brought with me, and I turned out the light. How many times had I set her name on fire? How many times did I remember and then let go?

Sleep came slowly like a branch on the waves, and I kept twitching myself awake. Fragments of dreams invaded my waking mind and I didn't try to stop them. New York began to smell like the island in memory, and the open window carried in the sounds of distant traffic. As I lay there I could see Suzanne's face staring at me over a coffee counter and Mike's from over a bar. Both of them were smiling wicked smiles and winking at my tired eyes. I missed them and their sarcastic grins, but they were far away in more ways than one.

Long black hair fell over Jane's face and I wasn't sure if the cigarette I smelled was from her breath or Paul's. Suddenly her hair was red, and when I looked down onto her painted toes she grabbed a pebble and flung it across the floor. She sat down at a piano and swayed as she reached into her purse to pull out a Lucky Strike, and as she lit it I found myself staring at the flame until finally I drifted off into sleep that was neither restful nor deep.

Chapter Nine

When I awoke the next morning the only real dream I could remember made me blush. Jane's face shimmered in my mind's eye as images began to be replaced by the vision of my room. We had been in a boat just outside the bay, lying back, absorbing the sun and talking about film. Her white dress was pulled down at the shoulder and up at her knees, and I could smell her skin. Our legs were intertwined and I couldn't remember much more. As I woke all the way up, what I could remember began to fade until all I was left with was a warm, flushed face.

I was up just in time to have breakfast with Paul and Stephen before they headed out, and it was good to see them again.

"How are you doing, James?"

Paul spoke so sincerely that I answered him honestly.

"I'm okay," I said, "but I had some strange dreams last night that made me wake up tired. How was your event?"

"It was boring, but I found some decent vendors and met a few nice people. It wasn't a complete waste of time, although the food could have been a lot better. It was mostly nice to see Mariko and her son. I don't think Stephen had a good time at all."

"I'm right here, Dad. And no. I didn't."

Issa continued eating the piece of apple she had in her

mouth. "Oh," she said between bites, "how would you feel if we invite Sebastien over for diner tonight? James and I will make something, and if you bring home a few bottles of the Domaine Drouhin, we'll be all set."

"Sure," said Paul. "If he's free we can bring him back with us on our way home so he doesn't have to bike out here by himself."

"Cool!" said Stephen, who had remained pretty quiet throughout breakfast. "I hope he's as interesting as he looks."

"Stephen!" said Paul.

"What, Dad? All I was saying is that he looks..."

"I know what you were saying, but don't try to set yourself up with expectations like that. It's rude and most often it's disappointing as well."

"Thanks, Paul," Stephen said sarcastically. "Now let's go so we don't miss the ferry. I would hate to be late for school. Again."

"Okay, okay, we're going. Hold your horses for a minute."

"I'll get the dishes, Paul," I told him when he started putting things away. Issa and I cleared the table as the boys got ready to head out the door. A few minutes later we sent them down the path with their bikes wobbling beneath them and the clear morning air and salty wind cool at their backs.

"Issa?" I said as they turned the corner. "Can I talk to you about something?"

"Sure, James!" I was glad to see she seemed to be in a good mood.

"I got a letter from Jane last night." Once again she didn't press me for information, but simply waited for me to continue.

"She's my ex. I know I've mentioned her, but this is sort of odd. She's going through a nasty breakup and she's wondering if she can come visit. We've mostly stayed friends since things ended with us, but I don't want to impose on you and Paul." I winced at my slight stretching of the truth, but I knew if I explained just how out of the blue this all was then Issa would be as confused as I was.

"Is this the woman who made it hard for you to write?"

There was no easy way to answer that. "Yes" was the answer, but the question meant more than that. She was really asking whether I would be able to keep writing if Jane came to visit. All I could do was nod.

"It sounds like it might make things difficult. But it's totally up to you. Do you want her to come?"

"I haven't gotten that far."

"Well, how do you feel about it? Would you like to see her? Does it sound like fun having her here, or does it feel like an obligation and a distraction?"

"I hadn't thought of it like that. I was mostly worried that it would be an imposition on you and Paul."

"This is your house as long as you're here, James. We like having you here, and you've been such a huge help I think we may need a James every summer to do the repairs. But think about it for a while and let me know. If you'd like her to visit, I'm sure it would be no problem with Paul and Stephen. If she was a girlfriend of yours I can only imagine she's lovely, charming, and delightful to have around."

Issa turned toward her studio. I walked over to the piano and sat down on the bench just staring at the keys. I was still somewhat dazed from my lack of sleep, and I could feel nervousness growing in my stomach. One finger touched the keys and a slow scale slipped out. When I finished I move up a half step and played the next scale still focusing on the ball of tension in my stomach. I tried to use my left hand as well and found that I couldn't cross my fingers over well enough to play more than five notes in a row without stopping to adjust my hand. When I reached the key of G, I began to actually relax. I eventually got it so both hands could play the same scale simultaneously with only a brief pause to adjust my fingers in the middle, and the anxiety in my stomach shrank to a slight irritation.

When I decided it was time to write again I headed back toward my room to grab a notebook. I peeked my head into Issa's studio on the way out, to let her know I was going. She was sitting on her stool in ripped shorts and an old tank top, and she waved me in from where she was sitting. I had been in her studio before, but only briefly, and I never had time to thoroughly look around. The floor and walls were lined with bowls and vases of every size and shape. There were molds of torsos standing upright, and I saw the shape of a chin and neck leaning against the wall on a shelf. Issa's wedding kiln, as she called it, was outside the back door to her studio, but today it was cold and empty. She was still working on her useless pieces inspired by my novel (which felt pretty damn useless as well), and they were each specifically designed to corrupt the function they appeared to fulfill. She had vases made with clay so porous that water would seep out, and beautifully shaped teacups with patterns punched into their bases like intricate latticework.

"Have you made a decision about Jane?" she asked without looking up from the wheel that was spinning between her knees.

"I'm going to write her this afternoon."

"What's the verdict?"

"I don't know yet. I assume I'm going to say yes, but I'll see what happens when I try to write the letter. Do you think it's a bad idea?"

"I'm not in a good position to answer that. Do you miss her?"

"Always."

"Well, that's something then."

I stood there fidgeting. I wasn't sure what I wanted, but the sound of Issa's voice made we wonder. I had to admit that I was falling for her in spite of myself, and suddenly I pictured Jane showing up and making everything more complicated. Did I want her to tell me not to say yes?

"I'm just beginning to feel like I belong here, and Jane always comes with challenges."

"I think you fit in well. Even Stephen is enjoying having you around."

"And you?"

She looked up and threw a shy smile at me.

"I can't imagine anyone I'd want more. I mean, as a guest," she said, blushing.

"Well, that's an endorsement I can live with. I'll let you know what happens. It sounds like she doesn't have much time off, so it may be a short visit no matter what."

"Like I said, it's up to you. Good luck with the letter, and let me know if you write anything else. I like hearing about it."

"If I get anything decent out of it, you'll be the first to know."

"I wouldn't worry about that. I'm perfectly happy with indecent as well."

It was my turn to blush as I gathered my things. I stood for a few minutes longer watching her work.

The wind through the window was cooler than it had been and the smell of clay reminded me of a pottery class I had taken in college. I watched the lump spinning under her fingertips slowly begin to take on the shape of a bowl. The lip grew larger and larger, and the hollow of the bowl began shrinking until the weight of the edge was too great and it fell away, leaving a mass of clay spread out on the wheel. Issa looked up at me as she began clumping the clay back into a ball, being careful not to leave any air pockets.

"I'll see you later this afternoon," I said. "Do we have everything we need for dinner tonight?"

"I think we're okay. I don't feel liking spending all afternoon cooking and I'm sure that Sebastien will appreciate whatever it is we make for him. Besides, who knows if he'll even be able to make it. If you don't see him at the café don't worry about it. I mean, nothing against having handsome Frenchmen for dinner, but the house is getting a little boy heavy, if you know what I mean."

I left through the back door and snagged the one remaining bicycle from the side of the house. I put my bag in the basket and headed off into town. Nothing says "serious author" like a bike with a basket.

The café was quiet when I arrived, and once my coffee was ordered I pulled out the letter from Jane and read it again. It brought up as many questions as answers, but it demanded a response. Calling would have made sense. Paul and Issa had a phone and there was decent service in town by the bay. I could even borrow a laptop and send an email, but none of those options felt right. I pulled my notebook out from the bag and twirled my pen in my fingers. I bit the cap between sips of my coffee.

Dear Jane,

The island is prettier than you can imagine and Paul and Issa with whom I'm staying are delightful. They have a smart fourteen-year-old who makes me feel simultaneously like an old man and a child. The house is small but warm, and the views of the ocean are amazing.

There's only one café in town, which is where I'm writing this letter, and they serve perfect coffee and good wine. You can watch sailboats come in and out of the harbor for hours at a time and there's so little to do it's infectious. The woman who owns it talks constantly about New York and she feels like she was carved from the white mountains themselves. You'll like her.

As for a visit, you're welcome any time you like. I feel so far away from everything down there that I'm not sure where we are or even where we left. I know that I miss you, and I know that I'd love to see you. I also know that we'll argue and possibly fight, and I want you to come anyway.

So, now that we've cleared that up, just let me know when you're coming. I'm sorry to put this down on paper rather than calling, but I figured it should be answered the way it was sent.

Love,

James

Without thinking I pulled the Zippo out of my pocket and flicked it open. I watched as the flame lit easily, and I had to stop myself from lighting the letter. I snapped it shut and stared at the pages in my hand. It hadn't occurred to me that writing back meant writing something down for real. It meant I couldn't delete it with fire and let myself forget it. Not only was I going to share something I wrote, but I was going to share it with Jane.

I folded it quickly and put it in an envelope. I wrote out her name and address on the front and fixed a stamp to the top right corner. Some things should be done without pause, I thought as I walked the two blocks to the post office and dropped the letter in the slot.

By the time I got back to the café, Abigail was gone, and Sebastien was sitting at a table smoking a cigarette and drinking a glass of wine. I tucked my shirt in as I approached him and he smiled and waved once more. Rather than going back to my seat, I headed over to his table. He pulled out a chair next to him.

"Hey, I'm James. Sebastien, right?"

"I've been here for two days and everyone already knows my name. This really is a small island."

"I know just how you feel. The first time I sat down Abigail came out, called me James and brought me a piece of pie and a cup of coffee."

"With cheddar cheese?"

"A fucking plate of it."

I leaned back on my chair and called the waiter over, ordering a beer and a glass. We both turned to look out over the harbor. There was a new boat tied up in the bay, flying a Canadian flag.

"So, where are you from?"

"I'm from Paris, but I work in Florence now. How about you? Is this your home?"

"Not yet. I'm from New York, but I'm up here for the summer. Trying to write a book."

"I won't ask what it's about. Is there anything worse than someone asking a question they don't really want to know the answer to?"

"You could ask and mean it."

"Or I could say it sounds like a lovely way to spend a summer and leave it at that. Besides, if we talk for a while, you'll tell me about yourself. We always come back to the things we care most about."

"Well, what about you? What brings you to our little corner of nowhere?"

"Only Americans need an excuse to travel. We Europeans just go. I've never been to Maine, and so I came to Maine. I like your seafood and your rocky coasts. Plus, you have good wine, beautiful people, and very little to do."

"You mean Melissa."

"Actually, I was speaking about you, but she's lovely as well. How do you know her?"

"That's sort of a long story without much of a beginning. I'm staying with her and her husband on the other side of the island. They have a small house with a view of the water and a porch that is completely divine. They do nothing but drink wine and throw pots. They cook and they paint the house over and over again, and if they feel especially motivated they tend to the garden."

"You are a lucky man. And I think they may be lucky to have you. It sounds like a perfect summer. I wish I could stay longer, but I only have a few days."

"Where are you off to next?"

"I have to go to New York for some work, and then I fly back to Rome next week. I wonder if I like New England because it's old. Most of your country is newer than my favorite restaurants in Italy, but up here, it feels old. There's something romantic about it."

"Abigail tells me that people have lived on this island for nearly four hundred years. I can hardly imagine living here now, but back then? It sounds impossible."

"As much as I like the idea, I think I would get lonely. I need people around me to survive."

My beer was almost gone, and I had hardly noticed that I was drinking it. Sebastien was so easy to talk to I had to resist pouring out my heart and asking for his opinions on everything. I knew that if I didn't get back to the house then dinner would never get made. And besides, there was a beautiful redhead who was starting to occupy far too many of my dreams.

"Well, that reminds me. We're having dinner out at the house tonight if you'd like to join us. I think you'll like them all and we'd love to have you."

"A home-cooked meal sounds wonderful. What time should I come find you?"

"Stephen and Paul get off the ferry around six. Why don't you meet them here and they can bring you out?"

He stood and took my hand again. His skin was warm and his grip was firm. He smiled as he said goodbye.

"It was really lovely to meet you, James. I'm looking forward to dinner."

I went to leave money on the table for the beer, but he

handed it back and insisted that it was unnecessary. I thanked him again, and began the long ride home across the island.

As I turned off of the street and onto the path out to the house, I thought for a moment of the letter I had just mailed. But Jane was so far away she almost didn't seem real. I shook my head and continued home.

Chapter Ten

We drank one bottle of wine as we cooked and we laughed more than we had all week. Issa touched my hand as we cut up vegetables, and I pulled strands of hair from her face as she leaned over the stove. We talked and talked about nothing at all as the evening came on, and I was happier than I had been in a year. I was home.

Towards the end of our supper preparation we heard the arrival of Paul, Stephen, and Sebastien. Their voices were loud and joyful as they cycled up the path laughing and talking in the cool evening air. Issa and I both walked out to meet them at the door. The three of them were quite a sight as they parked the bikes around the side of the house. We welcomed them home, and Issa and Sebastien were formally introduced for the first time. He kissed her hand when she told him her name, and she laughed and kissed his right back.

"Come on in," she told them as Stephen and I finished putting the bicycles away. Paul ushered us to the living room to sit on the couch while he opened the first bottle of wine.

"You have a lovely home," Sebastien said.

"It was my aunt's. Then she died, and now it's mine. It's the circle of life. And property law. And this is one of my favorite bottles of wine of all time. It's from Domaine Drouhin in Oregon and it's a fantastic Pinot noir."

Paul poured the wine for everyone, including Stephen, who was sitting on the floor leaning against the piano. Sebastien raised an eyebrow at it, but he closed his eyes after the first sip, and it was clear he was won over instantly. We ate our supper there, never bothering to move to the table, and it was easy and enjoyable. Sebastien told stories of traveling in Italy and Stephen peppered him with questions. Issa and Paul served food and wine without stinting, and by the time dinner was over at least two of us were on the far side of tipsy.

Stephen disappeared after dessert and the rest of us moved out to the porch. I found myself on the couch with Issa wedged between me and Sebastien, and it was delightful.

"You three look like you've known each other for years," Paul said as he lit a cigarette.

"Well, maybe we have. Sebastien and I spent at least an hour at the café this afternoon, and on this island that may as well be forever."

"And I know everyone," Issa said. "I mean, it is my island. Do you know that I haven't been to the mainland in four months? I think it's a record. Or maybe a curse. Anyway, the point is I can't leave."

"The point is you don't want to leave."

"I'm on the porch drinking wine, sandwiched between two handsome men. Why would I want to go anywhere?"

"If this was my home, I'm not sure that I could leave it either. Nothing against Italy, but this really is beautiful. I spend far too much time going from one place to another."

Paul crushed his cigarette out in the ashtray and for a while the four of us simply sat staring out over the water. I could feel Issa next to me, our arms brushing one another each time we moved. Sebastien's legs were crossed as he leaned back into the couch, and he took long sips from his glass. Paul finally got up with a surprising amount of energy.

"Well, unlike most of you, I need to get up in the morning for a conference call. So, I'm going to leave you three here with the last of the wine while I go see if I can find my bed. Sebastien, it was delightful to meet you. Please, don't get up and don't feel like you need to rush home."

In spite of the request, Sebastien did get up, and instead of shaking Paul's hand he pulled him into a brief hug with a kiss on each cheek.

"Thank you for having me. Your home is so welcoming."

"You're welcome any time. Now you kids have fun," he said before vanishing into the house.

And then it was just us three.

The breeze was almost too mild to feel, and the room was dark except for two candles. Issa poured the last of the bottle out into our glasses. We had been drinking for hours, and her words were nearly as blurry as mine. She pulled her legs up underneath her until they were crossed on the couch, and she leaned back enough that she could see us both.

"So, what is a girl to do. Here I am on the couch with two beautiful men, and my husband has left me all alone."

"Well, I'm sure he has complete faith in our intentions," Sebastien said slowly.

"Oh, I'm sure he does. Assuming you both intend to kiss me until I can't breathe."

I looked at Sebastien and he looked back with a raised eyebrow. Issa's eyes were closed and she had one hand on each of our knees. I had no idea what I should do, and even less idea of what I wanted. I had dreamed of kissing Issa for a week, but this was not how I expected it to happen. Sebastien, on the other hand, didn't wait for another invitation.

He leaned in, placed one hand on her cheek and kissed her so slowly I felt my heart skip a beat. His fingers ran through her hair, and I almost didn't notice her arm sliding around my back and pulling me closer. She pulled away from the kiss and turned to me without a sound. She touched my cheek and smiled shyly.

And then I kissed her.

Her mouth was warm and soft, and her tongue opened my lips with more force than I expected. My arms were around her in seconds, and I never wanted to let her go. Out of the corner of my eye, I could see Sebastien kissing her neck, and our arms brushed as our hands moved up and down her back. She squirmed on the couch, her legs now stretched out in front of her, and the sounds from her lips were enticing.

She moved back to Sebastien, and I didn't pause before moving down to kiss her cheek, her ear, and her neck. I placed one hand on her stomach, and she pulled it up under her shirt to cover her bare breast. I pinched a nipple between my fingers as she moaned into Sebastien's mouth, and suddenly she pulled away from us both. Her eyes darted back and forth between us, and there was nothing but want in her expression. In one swift motion she lifted her shirt off over her head and then pulled Sebastien down to her breast. His mouth opened as I stared in wonder, and the freckles covering her body never looked so beautiful.

"Kiss me," she growled, and I couldn't do anything but comply. I moved from her neck to her chin and back to her lips, and the room got warmer by the second. Her skin was smooth and her muscles strong from long hours at the potter's wheel. When I slid down to kiss her other breast she squeezed my shoulder and bit her lip to keep from screaming. I was so mesmerized by what was happening that it took me nearly a minute to realize it was Sebastien's hand in my hair and not hers.

We moved over her body, kissing one spot and then the next as she slipped lower and lower onto the couch. She reached down and unsnapped the buttons on her shorts, opening them just enough for a hand. As Sebastien and I touched her thighs, we stared at the tangle of red hair exposed by her probing fingers. I looked at him and then back at her, and his fingers caressed my face. Issa sighed again, and stopped moving completely. Everything slowed down as we stared at one another, and before I knew what was happening his scratchy face was against mine and I was kissing him. It was completely new. His tongue pushed into my mouth as he pulled me close. His lips were full and thick, and his breath was strong with wine and smoke.

Issa spoke. "Holy shit. That's the hottest thing I've ever seen."

We both turned and looked up at her, and I tried to hide my embarrassment with a laugh.

Sebastien moved back to her body, kissing his way up her stomach until he was between her breasts, and both our hands were back on her legs, holding them stretched open.

Her mouth was softer and slower than his. Her fingers were light as they ran down my cheek and her kiss was wet and gentle. I moved my hand up to her stomach and then slowly down until I felt the fabric of her shorts. I didn't stop as my fingers slipped beneath the elastic and white cotton, and she let out another sigh when I moved further down.

"Please touch me," she whispered before kissing me again with far more force than before. I pushed two fingers inside her as my lips touched hers, and she writhed and wiggled between us. Sebastien teased her nipples with fingers and teeth, and his other hand moved next to mine against her stomach. When I finally let her go, he quickly replaced me, and I watched in wonder as her hips bucked up to meet him.

"You two are going to make me come," she moaned, kissing him fiercely once more.

I don't how much time passed with us moving between kisses and bites on her body, but we took turns working our fingers inside her and rubbing against her where she moaned the loudest. We nipped her nose and kissed her cheeks, opened our mouths against her ears, and stared in awe as she moved between us.

It was Sebastien who finally pushed her over the edge.

In the middle of a kiss she began moaning into my mouth and didn't stop. I looked down to see her thrusting up against his hand, and she arched her back as she struggled to keep quiet. I pinched her nipple between two fingers as she wrenched her face away and pressed her arm over her mouth. Her orgasm shook through her like a wave. Sebastien never stopped. It was only when her shivering began to slow that she placed a hand over his and pulled him from her. She held him against her stomach and kissed us both as her breathing calmed down. Her eyes were glazed over, a look I had never seen before.

"Will you do it again?" she asked.

"Do what?"

"Kiss," she whispered. "Just once more. Kiss for me."

This time his lips were slow and our kiss was gentle. I touched his cheek, but the space between us was so full of tension and pleasure that it was overwhelming. She sighed as our lips touched, and I felt her hand on the small of my back. When we finally pulled away, she was grinning like a fool and her hair was a mess of curls on her head. She reached down and buttoned up her shorts before finding her shirt on the floor. We held it up as she slipped her arms back inside it, and suddenly she was cuddling between us on the couch.

"Why would I ever leave?" she asked no one in particular.

"I can't even begin to imagine," Sebastien said, brushing her hair with his fingers. "James, you are a very lucky man. And Issa, I believe you may be a lucky woman as well." His look made me blush and I felt years younger than I was.

"May be?" she asked. "I don't think there's any question about that at all. And if that's luck, I want more of it. There aren't even words."

I picked up the last sip of wine in my glass and swallowed it as I looked back and forth between them. She was definitely right. There were no words at all that could describe how I was feeling. And at that moment, it didn't seem like there was any point in trying.

An hour later when Sebastien left, Issa and I shared a kiss in the hallway that lasted forever. It was tender and warm, and I wanted to ask a million things I didn't have words for. I wanted to ask why and why now. I wanted to know what came next. Most importantly I wanted to know when I could kiss her again. But she ended the kiss with a finger to my lips and a smile that made me forget everything. We held hands as we walked towards my room, and she touched my cheek and kissed my chin before finally continuing down the hall.

My room was dark and the window rattled in the wind right alongside my mind. I didn't even know where to begin thinking and instead it all hit me at once. I pulled out my notebook, and I turned on the bedside light. I sat up enough to be comfortable and let it all come out with my pen.

I'm still hard. Both my cock and my heart, and I don't know which one to start with. I kissed her and he kissed her and me, and it's all such a tangle of red curls and confusion that any place I start is the wrong one.

Let's start with freckles and his eyes. Why his eyes? I didn't even notice them at lunch, and what was I thinking?

Let's start with her breasts and her thighs and his hand on my cheek. When did that happen? When did I say yes or not say no, and why is it so fucking hot in here?

I wrote a story in college about a man who said yes to everything. I thought it was exceptional at the time, but now I wonder. Maybe if I read it again I would cry and find anger instead of joy. Why was I so fucking stupid when I was young, and what am I now?

If I don't kiss her again I may lose my mind. And as for Sebastien, I don't even know where to begin.

I tore the page from my notebook and held it in my hand,

wondering whether to run down the path to the ocean and set it aflame over the cold water. I was tempted to burn it right there in my room, but the thought suddenly felt foolish rather than romantic, and I felt young and insecure rather than brilliant.

I was holding something I didn't want to let go of. I wasn't afraid of losing the memory, but the page was something else. It was a hint of insight and a spark of awareness. It was all the things I couldn't manage to think at the time. It wasn't just her kiss and his hand. It was both and neither and most importantly it was mine. The night was ours, but this? This belonged to me.

I put the page back into my notebook and closed it. I placed it back on the table beside my bed and turned off the light again. It was the second time in a day that I had left words on a page and I'd have to live with that.

I reached down beneath the covers and closed my eyes. I could smell them both on my hands and lips. I rolled over to my stomach and remembered the sounds of her sighs and release, following them toward my own conclusion.

Chapter Eleven

The next morning I found Paul sitting by himself at the breakfast table. He had a plate set for me and the coffee was hot on the stove. I poured myself a cup before sitting down next to him, and I tried to act completely normal, which means I was about as awkward and uncomfortable as I can be.

"It's okay, James."

"What?" I asked, looking up from my coffee with a start.

"You and Issa. And Sebastien too. She told me about it when she came to bed, and I just wanted to say that it's okay. You didn't do anything wrong."

"I didn't. I mean. I don't..."

Paul sat back in his chair and took a bite of his eggs. I thought of a million things to say, but not one of them made sense. I must have missed the class on how to talk to someone after making out with their wife the night before. Possibly my college didn't offer it.

"It's always a little funny to say to someone, but I'm glad you like my wife and I'm glad she likes you too. It would be super awkward otherwise. It sounds like she definitely had a good time."

"It was completely unexpected."

"Really? You two have been flirting since you got here."

"Sure, but she's married..."

"And open."

"Right, and open, but that's not something I really understand yet. And then there's Sebastien."

"Now that is unexpected. I'm actually impressed. Issa's often more reserved when it comes to these things, so it's nice to see her going a little crazy. She's been having a tough time since she broke up with Liz."

"That was the ex-girlfriend?"

"They broke up about a month ago and it's been hard. Liz lived in Boston, so it's not like they saw each other all that often, but they were close. They wrote letters and they spent weekends together. Liz was out here one weekend a month last summer and she was starting to feel like a part of the family. And then pow. It was over, and Issa was stuck out here by herself most of the time with no outlets and not many people to talk to."

"I'm still trying to wrap my mind around it all, but I can definitely relate to shitty breakups. Hell, mine was over a year ago, and I'm still freaking out about seeing her."

"Right, I almost forgot. Issa mentioned that she might come for a visit. Did you get in touch with her?"

"I wrote her yesterday."

"You didn't burn it?" He was smiling, but it still struck harder than I wanted to admit. I shook my head.

"Nope. I actually mailed the damn thing. I told her she'd love it out here and to just let me know when she might make it up."

"That's cool. I think Issa will like having another woman around here as well. Even if just for a week or two. I'm sure Stephen and I can be a bit much sometimes. Are you excited to see her? You said it's been a year, right?"

I nodded, though I wasn't sure. A year, two years, who knows. There were days when it felt like no time at all and days when I could hardly remember why we broke up. I still pictured her sometimes when I wrote, but her tears and her anger faded each time I let something go.

"I don't know what to think," I said. "I miss her and I still love her, and I'm only mildly terrified that we'll tear each other apart within the first day. And after last night, I don't think anything makes sense anymore."

"It's definitely not easy. But hey, maybe you'll have a new perspective on it. I mean, you made out with my wife and a handsome Frenchman less than eight hours ago. I would say that some things have changed."

"I still can't believe that you're just okay with it all. I mean, I know you are, but I'm not sure I get it. I keep wondering what it would have been like for me and Jane and the thought drives me crazy."

"This kind of relationship definitely doesn't work for everyone. But be careful. Once Issa's got her hooks in you, it's hard to get away."

"I don't even know where there is to go. Speaking of Issa, where is she?"

"They went into town to do some shopping. Stephen wanted to bike and Issa sounded like she needed some fresh air. I suspect she's going to stop in and say hi to Sebastien as well. She's always courteous that way. Speaking of which, she left you a note."

Paul handed me a folded piece of paper before getting up and rinsing out his cup. He did a few dishes, put away the eggs and butter, and with a wave and a nod he was down the hallway and back in his room before I could say a thing.

Hey Handsome. Hope you had sweet dreams. I know I did.
Xoxo,
Issa

I read it two or three times and couldn't help but blush. I rubbed my hands through my hair before walking out to the porch and falling down on the couch. I closed my eyes and remembered the night before in vivid detail. A small shiver ran down my back, and I had to be careful not to lose myself.

I finally got up, collected my writing tools, and walked out the back door. I wasn't ready to see Issa and Sebastien in town, and sitting at the café talking about our evening as if nothing happened was a recipe for awkward. As much as I couldn't get it out of my head, I needed to focus on something else if I was going to get through the day.

I get stuck when I write in the same place every day. I don't understand how some writers can sit at their desk for years at a time and crank out page after page of brilliant prose without once leaving the house. When I sat near the harbor I remembered the Hudson River. I thought of the ferries and the boats that most people ignore. I wrote about coffee and wine at the café, and down by the water I wrote about waves and memory. Watching the gulls made me contemplate flight, and the tide pools with their mosquito-ridden puddles of stagnant water brought up feelings of loneliness and sorrow. They were full of empty shells, hollowed out by the beaks of birds and dropped from heights that terrified me. The tall grasses that grew nearby made me think of nothing at all.

I sat down on the top of the hill and looked out over the calm water. The nearby islands looked like beasts rising out of the sea. One had a lighthouse, and one a summer home with nothing but a dock on stilts clinging tightly to the rocks. They were the places to go if our larger island felt too busy and too full of life. If you needed to be even further away from the world, then there was always the next island. There's always somewhere smaller, more remote, and less welcoming.

I opened my notebook and reread the few pages from the night before. I forgot about the details and the feeling of skin on skin. I focused on my words and my sentences like they were strangers I was meeting for the first time. I turned to a blank page and I tried again.

Jane looks over my shoulder as I write and it makes me more self conscious than if she were a judge for the Booker Prize. She says that she likes to watch, and since I get to see her paint, it's only fair. But I delete more sentences than I put down while she's here even though she never says a word.

One night she lights a cigarette, and I write an entire chapter describing the smoke as it leaves her mouth. For the rest of the night I wait for her to ask me about it. I wait for questions or thoughts, but they never come. We cook dinner and we watch a movie on the couch, but my writing is left behind without a word.

When I begin my new novel, "The Locksmith's Daughter," I make a rule. There is to be no looking on as I type. I need a room with a closed door and nothing else around me. Even coffee shops and bars make me nervous.

She accepts without a word, and for thirteen months we don't discuss it. We talk about the business side of my life, and we talk schedule and covers. She has dinners with me and my agent, but the book is a secret locked up inside me that only she can't access. It's mine in a way I don't understand, and as much as I cherish my solitude, I begin to long for her to ask me again. I need her interest and her excitement to keep me going. The longer it goes on, the more obsessed I become, and with each new chapter, the story is more and more about Jane...

I really needed to burn that one. There were four things in it that I didn't like and two things that were completely untrue. Why would I write something that was untrue? I pulled the Zippo out of my pocket and rolled the page up like a cigar. I lit one end and blew through the other watching the smoke build as the edges burned. Soon it was gone. I kicked the ashes down onto the rocks and watched the wind swirl around them.

When I lifted my head up I saw the ferry rounding Green

Island and turning into the harbor to drop off its passengers. It was a coming and going I had seen twenty times before, but soon the boat would arrive with Jane on it. The worry in my stomach returned full force. I was excited to see Jane. I wanted to see her and walk these rocky shores with her. But with her came the fear that with Jane in my world, I would never write again.

When I got to the café Issa and Sebastien were sitting outside drinking coffee. There was an empty plate in front of them and an ashtray on the table. Sebastien was leaning back in his chair as Issa leaned forward, and out in the harbor the ferry was arriving just as three billowed sails were drifting off into the horizon. I sat down at the table and they each took a hand without saying a word.

"Hello lovelies," I said.

"Hey handsome. How was your morning? Sorry I took off so early, but Stephen was jonesing to get out and I needed some fresh air to clear my head."

"She claims that she drank a bit of wine last night, but somehow that's not what I remember at all." Sebastien winked at me as Abigail put a cup of coffee down in front of me.

"Hi there, New York. Anything to eat?"

"Thanks, Abigail. I think the coffee is perfect for now."

We waited in silence until she walked back to the café. I could share most everything with Abigail, but this? I wasn't sure if I could share this at all.

"In case I wasn't clear last night, that was completely wonderful. I don't know about you two, but it was just what I needed."

"I think James and I are happy we could help. And Paul was..." He trailed off, and I jumped in before Issa could say a thing.

"He made me coffee and toast this morning. He said something about being happy that we kept his darling wife company."

"He's amazing," Issa said. "When we first got together and I told him that I loved him but couldn't be monogamous, I thought he was going to throw me out. I was positive it was a deal-breaker, but instead it was the start of a long conversation. He listened and then listened some more and he asked questions that had never occurred to me. We spent months reading books and talking to friends, and somewhere in the middle it began to make sense. He's like a rock, and I don't know what I'd do without him."

"And I always thought Americans were uptight about sex."

"Oh we are," I added. "Most of us can't even say the word without giggling. Look at me? I giggle just thinking about it."

"That's not what happens when I think about it." Issa blushed as she said it, and it all came back in one rush of excitement.

"You know I live right upstairs. If you two are interested in some more time alone. Not to be forward, but I'm leaving soon, and if last night was any indication of what everything else might be like, I'd be curious to find out."

Issa looked at me, but I had no idea what to say. His invitation was polite and simple. It was kind and exciting, and it sent more emotions through me than I was used to handling at once.

"I've never kissed a man before."

"Really? I would have never known," he said.

"I got to see your first? It was so hot I didn't know what to do with myself."

"And you?" I looked Sebastien in the eyes, hoping he'd take it from there.

"To be honest, I mostly date men, but the last year has been a whirlwind of change and nothing has stayed still. I've traveled non-stop and I haven't had time to connect with anyone at all. There have been a few woman in my life who I've loved dearly, and one or two that I've made love to, but it's strangely new to me. And this?" He waved his hand over both of us. "This is a different thing. You are both attractive people on your own, but together I can't resist you at all. You have such kindness towards each other, and so much desire that it draws me in until I never want to let it go. I feel like a visitor who is allowed to be a part of something bigger than myself, and I'm grateful that you've let me into your lives."

"And pants. Our lives and our pants."

"Well, technically just yours. James and I have been incredibly well-mannered when it comes to keeping our clothes on."

"I..." I looked back and forth between them, but I didn't know what to say.

"We don't have to go anywhere right now, James." Issa took my hand under the table and held it to my knee. "I don't think anyone is in a hurry."

"It's just all a bit new to me. And unexpected."

"I definitely didn't think I'd be hooking up with our boarder and a French tourist on my porch when the summer started. In fact, up until last night I thought you weren't interested."

"Me? I've been crushing on you since I got here. That very first morning I could barely talk to you."

"You see what I mean? I get to watch this," Sebastien said, waving his hand at us again.

I took another sip of my coffee and a deep breath.

"I should probably point out that Paul and I do have some rules." Issa was looking at both of us. Sebastien leaned back in his chair, while I could hardly sit still. She kept going.

"Mostly about safety. So, whatever happens up there, and James, there's no pressure for anything at all, it has to be safe. It's all about latex. Lots of latex."

"I wouldn't have it any other way," Sebastien said. "James?"

"Oh, yeah. Definitely. Safety first," I said, trying to sound calmer than I was. "So, if we did go upstairs, what would happen?"

They both looked at me with the same expressions I had seen the night before, and I was no longer sure if I was more excited or scared. I had opened a door to something I wasn't sure I could handle, but sometimes you have to suffer for your art.

"I think we'd start with a glass of wine and a kiss," Issa said.

"And then?" I asked.

"Well, you two took such good care of me last night, I think it would only be polite if I returned the favor."

I gulped. I shifted in my seat. I tried to adjust my excitement. I squeezed Issa's hand even tighter.

"So," I asked, "how do we get up to your room?"

Chapter Twelve

Issa and I walked home in the early afternoon with our hands entwined. My mind and my body were both exhausted, and I was in awe of what had just happened. I watched the rocks beneath my feet as I followed the familiar path, and every once in a while I thought I saw a scrap of paper left along the trail. I tried to count how many pages I had written just to keep myself distracted. Was I in short story territory or had I at least finished a novella in my week of writing? Either way, it all belonged to the island now, and I could never get it back.

Paul was still working in his room when we got back to the house, and Stephen was out wandering the island on his own.

"Do you tell him about things like this as soon as you see him again?"

"There are no things like this. But yes, we usually fill each other in pretty quickly. I'm not sure about this one, though. I mean, I need to tell him, but it still feels new and..."

"Personal?"

"I suppose so. It's not the sort of thing we've done before. Although after last night I don't think he'll be surprised."

"Surprised about what?"

Paul walked into the living room just as I was pouring myself a glass of water. I tried very hard not to jump at the sound of his voice. He looked back and forth between us and when we didn't answer his expression grew dimmer.

"Issa?" he asked.

"Can we go talk in the bedroom?"

And then I was alone for the first time in hours, with only myself and my memory of the afternoon to keep me company. They closed the door behind them, and I wasn't sure whether I was going to hear screaming, laughter, or moaning. It was a story that could definitely lead to any of the three, and I was at a loss to understand it. Once again I tried to picture Jane coming into our room and telling me about a similar morning, and it was nearly impossible. And yet here I was on the other side without a worry in the world. Where the hell did that awesome sense of responsibility go?

My bedroom was hot from the afternoon sun, and the window was rattling in the wind. I sat down and thought about nothing and everything all at once. For the tenth time I picked up the postcard on my bedside table, but this time I picked up the pen and made a decision. I would write a fucking note to Suzanne and nothing would stop me.

Dear Suzanne, I kissed a boy and I liked it...

That wasn't going to work at all. No fucking way.

Dear Suzanne, The weather is lovely and my new friends are very nice. I just ate the great American novel.

Right, because that was so much better. How do you explain a month on a postcard? How do you explain an afternoon or an evening? What do you tell your best friend in the world when you have too much to say and not enough words (or nerve) to say it? Should I say that I was writing and leave it at that? Should I tell her about Jane and Issa and Sebastien? Maybe Abigail was easier to fit in and a better story to begin with.

I tried again.

Dear Suzanne,

I have completely lost my mind in the best way possible. The coffee is strong, the weather is perfect, and it's possible that I'm in love.

Miss you lots,

James

I reread it again with a satisfied grin. That ought to leave her confused, annoyed, and hopefully at least mildly amused. She could take it as she might, and if I didn't get a phone call from Mike in the next week I'd be surprised.

I walked into the living room, leaving the postcard in my notebook on the kitchen table so I wouldn't forget to mail it. Just as I turned back to my room Stephen walked in the door with an excited look on his face.

"Dude, did you know that there's a cave on the island? I mean, like a big cave with a secret entrance and everything."

"I did not know that. What's it like?"

"Well, I haven't technically found it yet. But everyone says it's there, and I think I'm close after exploring last week. Want to go look with me? Or are you busy writing?"

"I just finished a postcard, and I think I'm about done for the day. How far is it?"

"I don't know. Remember? Haven't found it yet."

"Right, I forgot about that. Well, let's grab food for later, so we don't have to come back." We scrounged up two water bottles, some cheese and bread, two bars of chocolate, and a bag of butter-flavored pretzels. We threw them into a backpack and turned off the lights behind us as we headed towards the back door.

"Should we tell Dad and Issa?" he asked.

"They're in their room. I don't think I want to bother them. Do you?"

He shook his head and we headed out the back the door, down the path, and out onto the rocks. There were some clouds far out over the water, but otherwise the weather still looked good.

I followed Stephen down to the shore where the rocky coast formed a broken sidewalk that circled the island. The white rocks met the crashing waves and the scattered vegetation stopped where the stone began. The small purple flowers I had noticed when I first arrived were still blooming along the shoreline, and small stagnant pools of water buzzed with mosquitoes.

The gulls squawked loudly when we got too close to their babies, but we trudged onward across the rocks without regard for anything. The sky grew darker as the clouds got closer, but it didn't seem to bother Stephen at all. In fact, he didn't slow down as he made his way through the broken terrain, and while he easily climbed down breaks in the path and up the other side, I struggled to keep up as best as I could. Every once in a while we'd stop and look out over the ocean or watch the waves crashing against the rocks.

"How far is this damn cave?" I finally asked. We had been walking for over an hour, and I was painfully aware that I hadn't had breakfast or lunch.

"I don't know," he answered with that big grin that seemed to say, isn't this exciting? "I know it's out here, but I haven't found it no matter how hard I've looked. I think the tide has been high though. It's out now, so we can get down lower than I could last week, and I think we'll be able to see it. It's more fun this way, isn't it?"

"It would be if it didn't look like a storm was coming in, and if I had something in my stomach other than last night's dinner."

"Do you always complain this much? Let's sit over there and figure out where to go. I'm pretty sure it's nearby, so maybe we can strategize over brunch."

"I don't know if this counts as brunch. Brunch usually includes a mimosa and some sort of poached egg over culturally specific meat."

"Maybe in New York it does, but up here brunch is what

happens when you eat breakfast after six a.m. It's what happens when you pack a bag full of chocolate and eat it on the rocks because if you spend one more minute inside you'll never make it through the next winter."

"Holy shit," I said, stopping and looking out over the water.

"What?" he asked.

"I've never really thought about what it's like out here in the winter. It's so damn pretty, but you don't leave, do you? I mean, you're here all winter long and you probably don't see the sun for weeks. How the hell do you survive?"

"I've been asking myself that for two years. I like the snow and the cold, and I love sitting in front of the fire, but there's nothing worse than taking the ferry to the mainland at seven a.m. in February and wondering if you'll ever feel your fingers and toes again."

We sat down on a flat piece of rock and dangled our legs down over the crashing waves below. It was a fairly high vantage point, and we couldn't see a single building when we looked behind us. The rocks went on forever, and behind us were flowers and a few scraggly trees scattered about. We opened the bag and I took a long sip of water before finding the pretzels and cheese. Stephen started in on the chocolate, and as I looked out over the water I got more and more nervous about the weather.

"Are you sure we should be out here?" I asked.

"It's fine. It's just cloudy. They look different when it's going to storm. You can tell because of the horizon, and the wind doesn't taste like this."

"You're totally fucking with me."

"Maybe a little," he said and I couldn't help but laugh.

We looked down at the rocks in search of what might look like Stephen's cave, but it was hard to see anything without moving closer. We ate and discussed a few places to start searching, and I wondered what it would be like to write there. I wondered if I could light pages and where they would fall.

I finally slung the bag over my shoulders and climbed down towards the water to search for something I was nearly positive didn't exist. Stephen went up the coast; in seconds he disappeared behind the rocks and I had to focus on my own climbing. The rocks were wet and slippery the lower I went, but they did open up more and the hollow spaces in between them grew larger as I crawled about. I found a few holes that almost counted as caves, but nothing like what Stephen had described. Just as I was about to give up I heard a yell. I started in surprise, but quickly realized it was a yell of excitement rather than fear, and I made my way toward it. I came around the turn to where I was sure he had been and while I could still hear him, I couldn't see a thing.

"In here!" came his voice one more time, and I saw it: a dark opening in the rocks just barely large enough for me to fit through.

"Are you serious?" I asked as I crawled towards the entrance. "How big is it in there? I'm not climbing into a dark hole if it's just a wet, seaweed-infested pit."

"It's huge!" came his cry, and he sounded further away than I expected. Despite my better judgment, I leaned down and crawled through the space in the rocks. It was cold and wet for the first few feet, and I felt unbelievably claustrophobic as I made my way in. Before I knew it the rocks were dry, and when I looked up, I could see light from the darkened sky pouring through a small crack in the ceiling. I realized I could actually stand, and Stephen was sitting on a large flat rock on the other side of the cave.

"Isn't this amazing!" he exclaimed. I looked around and couldn't help but agree. It was far larger than I expected and the nooks and crannies went off in all directions. There wasn't much light, and from what I could tell the only way in and out was the hole we had crawled through.

"This is fucking cool," I said.

"I didn't believe it was really here. I mean, people talk about it, but no one's ever told me they found it, and I assumed they just meant it would be a little crawl space. But look at this! It's amazing, and it's dry. It's above the tide line, and you can just see the sky through these cracks. I wonder what we're under. I bet I've walked over this a hundred times and never noticed it before."

We were both so caught up in awe and wonder that we missed the first thunderclap. We heard the second one, and just as the third one hit, rain began to pour in through the same hole that let in light. We scrambled back towards the opening, but the sounds from the other side were just as frightening as the sounds above.

If you have never been on an island when a storm is coming on, it's difficult to imagine. The sky turns black and blue with streaks of orange if the sun is setting. The air gets thick and the birds dart about. The water begins to swell, and right after you see the first streaks of lightning in the sky, the whitecaps begin to glow. The white masts and sails on the ships begin to reflect a light from some unknown source and they shine with a bright passion you will never see anywhere else.

You can hear the rain before you feel it, and sometimes you can see it move across the water like a wave of its own.

When the lightning truly starts to fall it breaks up the sky like cracks in a glass. Sometimes deep and yellow, it bursts high in the sky, illuminating the clouds and the sea below. Other times it burns down in a spear of gold with a violent snap. The thunder is detached from the source, and the ground echoes with its deep vibrations.

"I don't think I can go through it," Stephen said quietly. He was trying not to sound afraid, but he was shaking and staring at the exit like it might bite him.

"I think the waves are crashing against the space we came

through." I was trying to sound calm as well, but the truth was that I was just as scared as he was, and the thought of crawling down the hole and out through the crashing waves and pouring rain didn't seem very enticing to me either.

"Is the tide going in or out?" I asked. He didn't seem to hear me, so I asked again much louder.

"It's going out," he finally said. "It's still going out!"

"So we wait. We can wait out the storm and then we can head back when the waves have calmed down and the tide is lower. At least it's dry in here, and even if the tide did come in we're probably safe. It may even be the safest place on the island right now."

We sat down next to each other, and we listened to the waves and rain and tried to think of something else.

"Do you think Issa and my dad are okay?" he asked.

"They're probably back as the house, closing the windows and shutters. I'm sure they're fine." I didn't have as much confidence in my voice as in my words, but it was the best I could manage. We didn't say anything for a while and both of us were lost in thought.

"Are you going to stay?" he finally asked.

"At least until the rain stops," I said.

"That's not what I meant. Do you think you're going to stay on the island? Is it going to be the four of us from now on, or are you going to just pack up and go back to New York and I'll never see you again? That's what happened with Liz, just when I got used to her being here. "

"Honestly?"

"That would be nice," he said.

"I'll be here for a while, but I don't really know. My friend Jane is coming to visit, so I'm not leaving anytime soon. I'm writing again, which is good, but I don't feel like I have too much control over what's going on in my life."

I tried not to think about my morning, and I especially tried not to think about his stepmother in my arms. I ignored her freckles and her kisses, and I definitely didn't think about her body pressed between mine and...

"Hello?" Stephen was waving his arm in front of my face.

"Sorry, I got caught up listening to the thunder. I don't know. This place is confusing."

"Are you in love with Issa?" he asked. It was one of those questions kids can ask and get away with, and I was almost mad at him for it. I took a few deep breaths and tried to do all the things I knew I was supposed to. I tried to pay attention to what I actually felt, and I tried not to get distracted by my gigantic urge to ignore the question.

"Well, I've only known her for a week and change, and I don't think I understand this whole open marriage thing any better than you do." I leaned back against he rocky wall. "I don't know how it happened, but I think I kind of loved her the first day I was here. The first time she sat next to me on the piano bench, and the first time I saw her with clay in her hands, I just couldn't stop thinking about her. She's pretty and smart, and..."

"And my stepmom. I get it, dude. I don't think I need to hear everything else."

"Sorry about that. Why am I talking to you about this?"

"I want to be in love," he said.

I sat up and stared at him. I had no answer for that at all, but I could sure as hell relate.

"I want to at least crush on someone. I want to have someone in mind I can't get out, and I want to smile when they walk into the room. I want to pass fucking notes in class, and I want to wait for him when school is over and let him walk me to the ferry."

His eyes were closed and it sounded like he was also saying this for the first time out loud.

"Him?" I asked. " I didn't realize you were into boys."

"Well, you don't ask too many questions, do you. Although I still think it's obvious. I always did."

"I'm sorry?"

"It's fine. I just want to hold someone's hand, and I don't want to feel weird or guilty for liking someone! I don't want to have to pretend that I don't care, and I don't want to worry what people think of me anymore. Shouldn't everyone get that?"

All I could do was nod my head. I didn't have any experience talking to a teenager, and talking to a teenager about love was even worse. My memories of my high school years filled me more with dread than anything else, and Stephen was in a whole different world.

He looked at me again and he eyes were red. There was nothing I could say, but I nodded over and over again before I finally put an arm around him. He leaned in against me for just a moment before getting up and walking back and forth in the darkness. The rain was still dripping though the hole in the ceiling and the thunder and waves sounded above us.

"It just doesn't seem fair. You all are so fucking happy, and cute, and in love, and I can't even find someone to flirt with!"

"Are you telling me there's no one at school that you even think is attractive?" I asked. He looked down as he paced and I grinned.

"So there is someone, you just don't want to talk about it."

"Because it doesn't fucking matter! What am I going to do? Ask him out for coffee? See if he wants to come out to the island and meet my crazy polyamorous parents? That'll go over well. This is my dad Paul, his wife Issa, and his girlfriend Mariko. James is here for the summer, but I don't know if I should call him uncle yet. I can't even talk about it with other people because they don't want me telling, and my parents are the last people I want to talk to."

"So, you can't invite him out here because you're afraid he won't like your crazy family, or because you're scared he'll say no?"

"Can it be both?" He sat down again. The storm sounded like it was getting worse.

"It probably can be," I said. "Look, I know I've been all wrapped up in everything as well, but I don't want you think that I'm on the other side. I mean, this is crazy to me too. I don't know what the hell I'm doing, I don't know if this whole poly thing is a good idea, and I don't know if it's going to work out."

"Can we keep talking about me?" he asked. Fuck, I'm the most self-centered person I know, I thought. Here's Stephen finally opening up to me, and I have to go on about my own shit.

"So, should I invite him out?"

"Is he gay?"

"No," he said. "At least, probably not. I mean he's just another kid at school and we talk a bit, but we're not even really friends. I just like the stuff he writes in English, and I like the doodles he makes in the margins of his books. I like the music he listens to and I like the clothes he wears, and he's nice to me and he smiles at me, and I can hardly fucking talk to him."

"Sounds like high school to me," I said.

"Is that supposed to make me feel better? Because I bet in high school you at least knew that the cute girls liked boys, and if they didn't like you then it just meant you just weren't quite cool enough. It's not like it meant you were a freak, or a weirdo, and maybe they teased you about it a little, but it wasn't like this."

"I was just trying to be supportive."

"Well, you sounded like a dick."

"Look, I don't know what the hell it's like to be you, okay? I don't know what it's like to live out here all year round, I don't know what it's like having parents that do what yours do, and I don't know what it's like to be gay. I wish I had better advice, but I say go for it. It's not like it's going to get worse, right? Invite him out here, and see what happens. Maybe he says no, and maybe he doesn't. Maybe he comes out and freaks out when he thinks you like him, or maybe he's flattered and becomes your new best friend. And maybe, just maybe he thinks you're cute and smart and likes your doodles too."

"Maybe he likes my doodles?" Stephen was laughing. I realized I'd almost yelled that last part.

"Okay, not the best choice of phrases," I said. "I just don't know what else to say. Either you go for it and find out what happens, or you just leave it alone and you sit around being miserable on your own."

"We should get stuck in caves more often," Stephen said as he put his hand under the small waterfall of rain. "This is the best conversation we've had since you got here. You've been so damn busy hanging out with grownups that you forgot how much more fun talking to me is."

"That is God's honest truth," I said. "How's the storm coming?"

"It looks like it's slowing down. It's not actually raining anymore, it's just dripping down from the rocks."

I walked over to the crack in the ceiling and looked up as the light got brighter. We walked over towards the way out and we were quiet as we listened to the sound of waves against the rocks. They still sounded threatening, but much less so than a half hour before, and we finally decided it was worth heading out. Just before Stephen crawled into the small passageway he turned to me and asked me one last question.

"Will you make sure we still hang out? I mean, even when Jane gets here, will you promise that we'll still be friends? At least while you're here."

"I promise," I said. "Whether I'm here or not."

Chapter Thirteen

Dinner was awkward. Paul and Issa were sweet and affectionate, but I didn't know where I belonged. Had they talked about our morning? Was Paul angry with me? I was completely in the dark and everything out of my mouth sounded clumsy and strange. Stephen talked constantly about the cave and our afternoon walk, but I couldn't think of anything to add. He told them about the storm and we sounded like brave heroes who had faced down a monster.

"I was worried about you," Paul told him when he was finished.

"That's a first."

"Well, I don't normally have to worry about you, because you don't normally go off in the middle of a storm."

"I wasn't alone."

"Which we didn't know," Issa added.

"I can take responsibility for that. He asked if we should tell you that we were going out, but you two were in your room, and I didn't want to bother you. I told him it would be fine."

"Well, I'm glad you're both okay. The storm did some damage in the harbor, and the café lost a few shutters. It was not a good time to be out on the rocks. Even if you were hiding in a cave."

"It was awesome, Dad. I mean, it's totally amazing. You have to come see it sometime, okay?"

"When it's not pouring down rain and there's no lightning."

"Yes, Issa."

The rest of the dinner was quiet, but I could read nothing from either of them. Paul looked at me with an expression I didn't understand and Issa didn't seem to notice me much at all. She held Paul's hand and touched his arm every chance she had. She leaned against him and refilled his wine glass whenever it was low. They looked happy, but everything felt unfamiliar. Even though I was surrounded by three warm people, I felt completely and utterly alone.

I wanted to talk to Issa, and I wanted to talk to Paul, but mostly I wanted to know that everything was all right. My nerves got worse and worse as the evening went on. I cleared the table and did some of the dishes in silence, but it was more than I could take. I finally excused myself just as they were moving out to the porch and made my way back to my room. I needed to write or I was going to lose my mind.

My notebook was still there, and there were pages left from earlier in the day. I didn't read a word as I closed my eyes and tried not to think of anything at all. I took two deep breaths, and then I wrote.

The day after I hand in the first draft of my novel, Jane tells me that she's pregnant. We're sitting on the couch and I have just opened a bottle of Thomas Hardy Ale I've been saving for the occasion. She doesn't lead up to it. She doesn't warn me or give me any hint of anything at all. I pour us both a glass and she simply moves it to one side.

"Oh, James, I forgot to tell you that we're going to have a baby."

"That's funny," I say.

"I don't think it's funny. It's think it's slightly fucking terrifying, and I'm not sure what we're going to do, but none of that makes any difference. I took the test this morning."

I put my glass down and stare at her. She isn't laughing and she isn't joking with me.

"You're serious."

"Of course."

I wrap my arms around her and I hold her. I kiss her hair and I try to think of something brilliant to say, but nothing comes out at all. A baby. James and Jane are going to have a baby?

I closed my notebook and looked down. I was crying once more, and I couldn't hold it back. My tears and sobs grew stronger with each minute, and I had to cover my mouth to keep from calling down the house. I pulled the Zippo out of my pocket and flipped the lid open, but there was nothing to do. I was stuck in my room and there was no way I could move. My body was tired and sore from climbing on rocks all afternoon, and my head wouldn't let me go.

When I stopped trying to hold back, everything came out at once. My nose ran and the tears wouldn't stop. My legs and arms shook as I clutched them to my chest, and even my breathing was impossible to control. I rocked back and forth on the bed, and I cried and cried until I could no longer feel a thing.

When I was finally able to stand up, there was a knock on my door. I wiped my eyes and tried to straighten my clothes.

"James, can I come in?" Issa's voice was quiet.

"Of course," I whispered.

I was sitting on the edge of the bed when she entered, and she starting talking before she saw me.

"Hey, sorry about dinner. We didn't mean to get on your case about the storm, but we were super worried."

"No big deal," I said, trying not to look at her.

"And also, about this morning..."

"How did it go with Paul?"

"It was a little challenging, but it ended up in some insanely hot sex. I think he was more surprised than anything, and that always makes things hard. But we talked through it, and somewhere in the middle he went from being nervous that I would run off to France with you, to so turned on that he didn't let me leave the bedroom for... James, are you crying?"

I hadn't meant to look up, but I was listening and it happened all the same. I shook my head, as if that could explain away the tears and the red eyes, but without another word she was sitting next to me on the bed. I wrapped my arms around her and the tears started up once more.

"I'm fine. At least I think I'm fine. I'm just having a moment."

"I didn't mean to come barging in here with everything, I just thought you would want to know. You were worried on the way home..."

"I did want to know, and I'm glad. It was hard not being able to talk about it at dinner. But then I came in here and started writing and thinking about Jane coming to visit, and I lost it."

Behind me, my notebook lay open on the bed, and I reached over and closed it. I didn't want anyone to read those words, especially not Issa. Not now.

"Do you want to talk?"

I shook my head and tried to force a smile.

"I'll be fine. I just need some time alone. It's been an intense day."

"I hope it wasn't all bad," she said.

I leaned in, and wrapped my arms around her again. Images came flashing back in an instant and in spite of myself, a shot of excitement ran through my body. I kissed her hair and her cheek and she held my hand.

"I think it's safe to say that the first half of my day was amazing. Mildly confusing, but amazing. I can't even begin—"

"You don't have to. I'm just glad that's not what's bothering you."

"Oh God no. But maybe we can talk about it tomorrow?"

"Of course we can." She kissed me on the forehead before

standing up and heading towards the door. She turned and looked at me once more and I sat up in bed.

"I am very happy that you're here, James. For more reasons than I can begin to count."

"Thank you," I said, before she closed the door behind her. I could hear her feet on the hard wood floors as she made her way back to her room, and for a moment I was present and nowhere else. I tried to hold on and stay there, but my hand brushed my notebook and brought me back into the past. Without thinking, I tore the last few pages out and stuffed them into my pocket. I grabbed the Zippo off the table and left my door open behind me.

The storm was gone, leaving the water calm and the wind cold. There were still a few drops of rain falling around me, but I didn't care. I stood there on the shore, looking out over the water, and I pulled the crumpled pages from my pocket. I lit them one at a time and I watched them burn. I dropped them still burning into the cold sea, and then hugged myself as the wind blew around me. The ocean was dark, and the water splashed against the rocks with a sound that was completely familiar and yet offered no comfort at all.

Chapter Fourteen

Mornings in Maine are almost always cold, and the next few days brought more rain and wind. I bundled up in sweaters when I got out of bed in the morning, and wrapped myself in blankets when I sat on the porch. The four of us stayed inside for much of it, and even when we did venture out to the porch we never stayed long. Issa and I managed the trip to the café only once, and while we had a glass of wine with Sebastien we didn't return to his room. I went to bed early and slept late, and every day I wrote more about Jane.

One morning I woke up tired, without the energy to undress for the shower. It was slightly warmer, and all I could think of was hot coffee and the porch. It was deserted when I sat down with a mug and a sheaf of horrible memories from the night before.

I put my feet up on the table as I looked out at the rain, and I wondered what the weather was like back in New York. Suzanne was probably already at work and Mike was sound asleep. I had no idea where Jane was even living, and I wasn't sure what I wanted to know. I read in the paper that the summer had been exceptionally hot so far, but all I knew of it was a few hot afternoons and nights when it was nearly too warm to sleep.

I finally pulled my notebook out. Maybe if I focused on the present the rest would feel less important. I let my mind drift back a few days to my morning with Issa and Sebastien, and all I could I remember was the feeling of skin on skin. There were lips, and hands, and red wine. Everything poured out easily onto the page.

From Sebastien's apartment I can see even more of the harbor. The boats are bobbing on the waves and the flags are blowing in the wind...

I wrote down everything. I tried to add emotion as well as touch, and my pages filled with vivid description. I moved between excitement and confusion with equal ease; it was a strange experience. I had moments of worry as I described their bodies, but I tried not to guess and I left out most of what I didn't know. I read my words a few times when I was done, and I tore them from the notebook. Blood moved through my body in very good ways, and I folded the pages and slipped them into my back pocket, thinking maybe some writing has a purpose.

"Writing about me?"

I nearly jumped when I heard Issa's voice, and my blush must have given me away.

"I was joking, but from that look on your face, I can make a few guesses."

"A writer takes inspiration where he can get it."

"Do hot threesomes count?"

"You count."

She sat down next to me and without thinking I wrapped my arms around her and kissed her. It wasn't a kiss leading to anything, but it was strong and warm and it made my heart leap in my chest. I still couldn't believe that it was allowed, and I was completely unsure of how to behave with her when it was just the two of us. With Stephen home from school we didn't have as much time alone, and even when we did I felt unsure. We had flirted for weeks, but our physical relationship was all wrapped up in Sebastien, and somehow it felt safer that way.

"I like you," Issa whispered.

"That's good to know. I don't think I've quite wrapped my mind around any of this."

"Are we confusing you?"

"It's not a matter of confusing. Okay, maybe a little, but mostly I'm trying not to guess about where it might go. Is this mostly just sex for you and Paul? I mean, I know he has a girlfriend, but I don't really understand what that means in this context."

Issa sat up and faced me. She pulled her hair back and tied it tightly behind her head.

"Our other relationships are just like any other relationship. Sometimes they're about love and connection, sometimes they're about sex, and sometimes they're more about friendship. The point is that we let ourselves get into other relationships without trying to put them into boxes and without limiting them. So, if Paul finds someone he has great sex with but that's it, then they get to do that. And if I fall head over heels with a girl from the mainland who can't figure out what she wants until it's way too late for me, then that's what I have to deal with."

"When did you two break up?"

"A few weeks before you came."

"You don't have to talk about it, I just don't really know the story. And it's been coming up a lot."

"I'm not sure what there is to say. She was wonderful and crass, completely unlike Paul. She was loud and dramatic and she made me laugh until my sides hurt."

"How long were you together?"

"Over a year. It was a challenge to see each other all that often, but she started coming out here on a regular basis and it was perfect. Stephen liked her and there were moments when I wanted to ask Paul if she could stay with us."

"What happened?"

"She had a partner at home right from the beginning, but I never met her. I never knew exactly how open they were and what was happening at home. She told me everything was fine, there was nothing I needed to know, and I was always too scared to push. Maybe I should have insisted that I meet her partner, or at least talked to her on the phone. I don't think she was lying to me, but it was somewhere in between." She shrugged.

"And then suddenly last month it was over. She called me the day before she was supposed to come for a visit and said she was going to make it work with her partner. She said she need a 'real relationship.'"

"Ouch."

"Yeah. Talk about a slap to the face. I sometimes forget how much pressure there is to do things a certain way."

"I'm sorry." It was the only thing I could think of to say. Issa crawled back onto my lap without another word. I let my hand rest on her shoulder and for a long time we simply stayed there on the couch, both of us silent and far away in our own little worlds.

"Sebastien leaves tomorrow morning." She sounded matter-of-fact.

"Do you want to see him again?"

"I think just to say goodbye. He's nice and he's fun, but I don't think it would be the same without you. Do you want to see him again?"

"I don't know. He makes me nervous and excited all at once, but I'm not sure I could do that again. It was hot, and it was fun, but I'd rather focus on us."

I nearly bit my tongue as the words slipped out, but Issa simply grabbed my hand and held it to her chest. She nodded before kissing my fingers.

"Maybe we can go have a drink with him later," she said.

"He is somewhat convincing. We'll have to be careful."

"He's too handsome."

"I think I'll take that as a compliment."

"I just mean that he knows it. He can travel the world and sleep with whomever he wants without ever having to deal with the consequences. Not that I'm complaining. Those were two hot fucking scenes. And seeing you two together was insane."

"I still can't believe I did that," I said.

"I can't believe you had never done it before. Not that everyone has been with another guy—in fact, I'm pretty sure Paul never has—but you seem open to it. Or at least you went along pretty easily."

"Are you saying I'm easy?"

"I'm saying you were up for the ride, and it was ridiculously hot."

"I probably would have done anything to make out with you. And watching the two of you gave me feelings. Lots of them."

"Like what?" she asked, looking up at me.

"I don't know, like jealousy and a giant hard-on?"

"You were jealous of us? He was way more into you than me."

"It didn't matter. And don't get me wrong, I liked watching. It's just that it was difficult as well. It's all a bit of a jumble right now."

Issa nodded and stayed exactly where she was, and it suddenly hit me that I had no idea what was next. Could I spend a night with her? Could we go on vacation? What would Stephen think? Would Paul come in at any moment and suddenly it would all be just a dream?

"Is it going to be strange when Jane gets here?" Issa asked. And then there was that.

"It's always strange when Jane is around, but probably not any stranger. I'll just tell her that I'm, um..."

"What is it?"

"I'm not sure what we're doing. I was going to say I'll tell her I have a girlfriend, but that didn't sound right. That I'm sleeping with a married woman, and her husband is in the next room?"

"We don't usually do that. I mean, the next room bit. It's too creepy."

"And everything else?"

"I don't know either, but I do know that I like you, and I want to spend more time with you and get to know you better. I also know that you're not poly, and this is all sort of new to you, and I don't want to pressure you into something you're don't really want."

"If you get any more amazing I'm not going to know what to do with myself."

"I'll try to tone it down a bit."

"So, what do you do on a rainy day?" I asked, after a long moment of silence.

"I sit in front of the fire and read. Or I drink tea on the porch. Or I roll around naked in bed all afternoon after a super hot shower."

"We can make a fire?"

"You can make a fire. And I can sit on the couch and watch you. And then we can cuddle and you can kiss me some more and tell me what dirty things you were writing about me."

The day drifted by slowly and we did as little as possible. We did make tea and a fire, and we alternated between reading on the couch and kissing like we were in high school. Stephen came out once as I was poking the fire and he made a sandwich as loudly as possible without actually saying a thing. I tried to get him to come hang out with us, but he grunted and walked back to his room.

In the middle of the afternoon I did something that surprised me.

"So, remember when you walked in this morning? And I was blushing."

"When you were writing sexy things about me?"

"Yes. That time. Do you want to read it?"

"Are you serious? I would love to."

I reached into my back pocket and pulled out the folded up papers.

"You have to promise me one thing," I said. She nodded. "You have to promise to be nice. I haven't written anything in a very long time and it's been even longer since I've shared anything with anyone. So, you can read it, but you have to be nice to me.

"Give it here," she said, grabbing the pages playfully from my hand. "I promise."

I watched as she opened them, and I could see her eyes begin to move over the words.

From Sebastien's apartment I can see even more of the harbor. The boats are bobbing on the waves and the flags are blowing in the wind.

Inside there's an open bottle of white wine and more tension than I can handle. Sebastien is smiling at us both with a grin that means just one thing, and I'm not even sure where to start. I don't know what I want, other than Issa's lips against mine, and I definitely don't know where I want it to start.

She's pulling me to her. I had one sip of wine and now her mouth, and he's standing there watching. I'm trying not to look at him, but his presence is strong and his eyes are penetrating.

Her hand is on my cock and I'm going to burst. She's pressing her palm against me through my pants, and she's kissing my neck. I can barely handle her touch, but her words are even more impossible.

"I'm going to make you come. Both of you," she says, looking over her shoulder. "I want to feel you grow hard, and I want to feel your bodies pressed against mine. I'm going to kneel right here and I'm going to..."

Her mouth is on my ear and her fingers are sliding my zipper down. Sebastien is moving closer and she's moaning as he presses into her from behind. She tilts her head back and kisses him, her hand never leaving my cock, and if something doesn't happen soon, I'm not going to make it.

"Take off your shirts," she says as she steps back to the bed. She lies down with her feet towards the pillow and she looks up at us.

Sebastien nods at me and begins to unbutton his own. I pull mine off over my head, and Issa's eyes are moving over us both with a hunger and a joy that I love. He stands next to me bare-chested, and we look at her together. He reaches a hand out to my stomach, but he pauses with a question.

"Can I undo your belt?"

I nod as Issa crawls closer to us on the bed, and before I know what's happening he's opened my pants and he's sliding them down to the floor. I reach over to him and do the same, and my hand brushes his cock, which is hard beneath his jeans. Issa's hands are on both of our waists, and with one step we are standing in front of her wearing nothing at all.

She's sitting on the edge of the bed now and she has me in one hand. She has him in the other, and I don't know if I feel more jealous or aroused. I try not to compare as we grow harder in her hands, but I can't take my eyes off him. Without warning he kisses me and everything else goes out of my mind.

"Wow. I think I may need a cold shower. Did I really say those things?"

"Are you finished?"

"No!" she said, as she snuggled down into the couch and turned to the next page.

In the middle of his kiss I feel her mouth on me for the first time. At first it's just her lips as both hands move to me, and then it's her tongue and her mouth, and everything has changed. Sebastien breaks our kiss and looks down in amazement as Issa takes in my cock, and his groan is audible as his hand moves down around his own.

I try to stand still as she holds me there, but it takes every effort I have not to fall. Sebastien puts one hand on my shoulder as the other moves faster and faster, and everything she does to me is amazing. When she releases me with a pop and looks up into my eyes, I see that look of lust that I remember from the night before.

I reach over to Sebastien, and with a kiss on his cheek I slide my hand down his body until he lets me wrap it around him. It feels strange and familiar. He's hard and soft, and it's nearly like my own.

"Can I suck him too?" Issa asks, and all I can do is nod, and pull him closer. Why did she ask me? I have little time for wondering.

I sit down next to her on the bed as she opens her mouth, and I'm aware that my feelings are bigger than I can handle. Is that envy or just confusion? Is there anywhere else I'd rather be? She licks him from bottom to top and she wraps her fingers around him as I stare at them both in awe. I feel disconnected from my own body, and I find myself holding her hair back so I can watch.

Without a word she stops, and she rolls onto her back and begins frantically pulling off her clothes. Her shirt ends up on the floor, and her jeans are on his pillow. Her bra and underwear disappear just as quickly, and she stands up between us and kisses me so hard I nearly yell.

I can taste him on her lips and mouth, and he pushes all three of our bodies together. I'm hard against her stomach and he against her ass, and for a while I pretend that I don't know which one I'm kissing. After long moments when all I want to do is thrust inside her, she steps to one side, and he pulls me in for a kiss again. This time our cocks touch, and I nearly jump back. His concern is covered with desire, but it's there all the same, and he lets me take my time as I move back to him.

"What do you want?" he asks.

"I want to taste you," I whisper, and he moans out a plea that can be heard across the island.

I'm sitting on the bed with a man I hardly know standing in front of me. There's a naked woman I adore sitting next to me with her hand on my cock and my mouth is open.

"Is this really what we did?"

"No. It's what I remember. Or maybe just how I want to remember it."

"There's more," she said, looking up at me. Her left hand was on my knee pulling me to her, and she was breathing grew faster with each sentence. The flush in her cheeks was the best compliment I'd had in years.

I hold him in my hand as I lean in closer, and I'm not sure if I can do it. It's not a matter of taste or desire, it's just fear of failure. Uncertainty mixes in with envy and worry at all the same time. But I open my mouth and he moves forwards until my lips close around him. I hold him firmly in my hand as Issa breathes into my ear and whispers filthy things. I take in more until I need to stop, and I let him out of my mouth with a pop and a grin. He's looking into my eyes with affection that I'm not sure I deserve.

"I think I could come just from watching," *she says.*

My cock is in her hand, and when I open my mouth again she does the same to me. I try to focus, but everything is happening at once, and he's struggling not to push harder and faster into my mouth. Issa never slows down and I try to learn from what she's doing, but I don't have the ability. There are so many places to kiss and ways to touch, and I want to try them all.

Until she says something new.

"Will you fuck me?" *she asks, sitting up next to me.* "Will you fuck me while I suck his cock?"

She has a condom in her hand, and I don't even say yes out loud as I kneel behind her on the bed. She lies down, and I watch once more as she takes him into her mouth. My fingers touch her ass as I roll the latex down over myself, and I pray that I will last.

I push her legs open with my knees and kiss the back of her neck.

"Are you ready?" *I whisper, as if I didn't know the answer.*

"Yes," *she moans.* "Please fuck me. Please."

"Fuck her, James," I hear as I'm struggling to find the right angle.

When I push inside her I forget about everything else. I forget someone is watching, and I forget what her mouth is doing. All I know is her body is strong beneath me and she's moaning and screaming as I enter her, and I love her with everything I have. I want to be there forever and I want a million other things I can't describe.

"I'm going to come," he says, breaking my wandering thoughts. I push her hair to one side of her back as I kiss her neck and thrust faster and harder inside her. She pushes back onto me as she grips him tightly in her hands and she tells him to come over and over again. She begs and she pleads, and it's too much for me to handle. I watch as he comes, and I can see her trying to swallow everything, even as I'm kissing her cheek and growing soft inside her.

She held the paper in her hand and I trembled next to her on the couch. It felt like forever before she spoke.

"You love me?"

"Artistic license. It made it a better story. I plead the Fifth. No idea what you're talking about." I was talking fast, and she was wrapping her arms around me like she didn't care at all what I was saying.

"I think I want a copy," she whispered into my ear. "So I can pull it out when you're not here and spend some time alone with it."

"It's not terrible?"

Issa put the paper down and climbed onto my lap. She kissed my mouth and wrapped her arms around my neck. I could feel her chest rise and fall as I stared at her, and I was once again amazed that she was there with me at all.

"It was almost as hot as being there with you. And I like hearing what it was like from another perspective. But I'm sorry that you didn't come. We'll have to fix that soon."

"I like that idea."

"Have you always written about sex?"

"Sometimes I think it's a way out. I used to write letters in college and I filled more notebooks with dirty thoughts than anyone should, but it's always felt like cheating. If I make the story dirty enough, then maybe no one will notice anything else."

"Or maybe we just write about things we like."

"I like that explanation better."

"I always make what I most want to make. For a while I struggled because I told myself that I needed to follow assignments. I wanted to learn how to make teacups so I tried it for two weeks no matter what I felt like doing. And you know what? It didn't work. I got better at it, but it changed it from play to work, and there's a reason I don't have a job right now."

"I've spent the last ten days trying not to write things. Which is funny after all that time I spent trying to write anything. But maybe you're right. Why not write what feels best?"

"Especially if it's sex. And if I can read it."

Her kiss lasted much longer than before, but I was far too aware of Stephen in the back room to stay focused. I kissed her neck and her collarbone before gently moving her off my lap and back onto the couch.

"If we don't stop now, then Stephen is going to walk in on something he probably doesn't want to see."

"If we don't stop now, Paul might do the same. I can't believe how much I want you again. And next time I want it to be just us two, okay? And I want to make you come so hard you won't be able to write a word."

"Is that a promise?"

"It's a threat, James. A very serious threat."

I kissed her again before getting up to poke the fire. We left one window partly open, and the breeze coming in from the rain balanced the heat of the fire perfectly. I spent enough time kneeling on the hearth to gently come back to my senses.

By the time Paul got home, we had opened the first bottle of wine, and the rain outside had gotten worse. He was drenched to the bone when he walked into the house, but we put more wood on, and after he changed his clothes the three of us lounged about over dinner and more wine. Every moment of awkwardness I kept expecting didn't arrive, and Issa moved between the two of us without a hint of regret. It wasn't until I stumbled back to my room at the end of the night that I realized Sebastien was leaving in the morning and we hadn't once thought to go visit.

I crawled into bed with my notebook in my lap and I opened it to a clean blank page. I could still taste Issa on my lips, but as hard as I tried I couldn't find the words. But I didn't have to force things. I didn't have to struggle with things I couldn't write. My day drifted through my mind as I tried to find a story, and each time I touched the pen to paper all I could think of was Jane.

"If we have this baby you're going to have to get a real job," she says to me. She's standing in the shower and rubbing her stomach. She's not showing at all.

"What do you mean if? I thought we were having a baby."

"Babies are a lot of work."

"Jane, I know that. What are you talking about? Are you changing your mind?"

"I haven't made up my fucking mind enough to change it. All I know is that it's a lot of work, and your parents are not going to pay for college. Again."

She's getting out and she's laughing but I'm not sure why. I don't have the nerve to ask her. When she bends over to dry her toes I wonder for a moment how long it has been since we've had sex. If she's two months pregnant, then it can't have been that long. Maybe I'm forgetting something.

These words aren't good for anything. Sometimes when I'm writing I can think of a purpose. Maybe I'm purging, or maybe someday a person will read them and laugh or at least smile.

Maybe it will change someone's mind, even if for just a moment, and the world will look different. But these words are just a mess of memories. They're not fit for anyone or anything at all. Still, I don't stop.

Jane hasn't come home. I don't know where she is, or what she's doing, but it doesn't matter. We've been fighting for a week and now we hardly talk. She turns around everything that I say, and I can't do a thing about it.

I'm drinking more than I should. Which is a lot. Scotch is good and who the fuck needs ice? I don't need to think anymore, and I don't need to fucking worry about her. She can stay out all week for all I care. I drink more and I open my laptop without thinking.

I open my novel to the last page. I can barely read the last page, but I don't care. What came before doesn't matter.

"She can fuck the whole city for all I care." I blink as I try to read the words. I keep writing.

I tore them out of my notebook and didn't bother to read them again. I got quietly out of bed and walked into the living room. The fire was mostly out, but a few red hot coals still lingered beneath the iron grill. I blew on them and watched as they grew brighter and hotter. I wedged my pages in between the bars and they burst into yellow and blue flame. It only lasted for seconds, but the color was bright and alive. I would smell the smoke in my hair for days if I didn't scrub it all out.

I closed my eyes as I lay back in bed, and I said Issa's name over and over again as I tried to fall asleep.

Chapter Fifteen

Issa and I went back to the café the next morning to say goodbye to Sebastien. It was like waking from a dream as we sat outside drinking coffee and eating breakfast. The sun had finally returned, and while the morning was cool it was promising to be a clear and perfect day. Abigail sat for a moment when she brought out breakfast.

"New York, tell me about the High Line. I hear they've turned it into a park."

"I'd like to see that," Sebastien injected.

"It's lovely. Long, winding, and narrow, and full of tall grasses and wild flowers. I wish they'd build one all over the city so I'd never have to walk on the street again."

"I'll have to visit this evening. It sounds like a good way to readjust to city life."

"I can't believe you'll be in the city tonight. It feels like light-years away."

"The world gets smaller every day."

Abigail sat for a moment, but before long she was distracted by the café and she disappeared inside, leaving the three of us alone once more.

"I'm sorry we didn't get out here last night. The rain was a bit ridiculous."

"I would have come visit you, but I kept picturing the two

of you keeping each other warm and I didn't want to break the spell. I'm just passing through, but you two look like you might be stuck together for a while."

Issa leaned back and looked at the two of us, smiling.

Sebastien's ferry was at eleven, so there was no time for much of anything beyond coffee, a bite, and a few words of thanks. Just before he left he hugged us both and kissed our cheeks.

"If you're ever in Florence, let me know. I would love to entertain you again."

We walked him down to the dock and waved our goodbyes as he shouted "Au revoir!" We stood for a long time watching the boat move out of the harbor and into the open ocean towards the mainland. Maine was a long strip of land on the horizon, and it seemed to stretch on forever in either direction. As the boat got smaller, we finally made our way back to the café, our fingers entwined once more.

We biked back to the house just after noon and Stephen met us at the door. He was on his way out to the rocks and he stopped us as we were putting the bikes away.

"You got a phone call, James."

"I did?"

"Yeah, Jane called. She wanted me to tell you that she's coming up the day after tomorrow. I didn't know what to say, so I just told her I'd pass it on. Also, Dad and I are going to the mainland tomorrow. So if you want us to meet her on the ferry we can. He promised to take me to a movie, and he says we can stay with Mariko and Tak again."

"Thanks, man."

"Whatever," he said, before taking off down the path.

"Well, that was quick," Issa whispered.

I took her hand once more, swallowing hard, and together we walked inside. She had work to do in her studio, and I was ready to get back to my writing, but we stood by the front door for a long time without anything to say.

"Do you think she'll like me?"

"I can't imagine anyone not liking you."

"That's not an answer. I don't know what her expectations are, or yours for that matter, but I don't want it to be strange. I know it's a new thing."

"I think we'll be fine. She's a good person. She's mildly crazy and sometimes loud, but she's sweet and she's brilliant."

"Okay. Just let me know if I'm getting in the way."

"Issa, there's nothing to get in the way of. I don't know why she's coming other than to get out of the city. I've hardly seen her in the last year, but we have talked and written a few letters. I think she just needs a break, and maybe being with someone familiar will be easier for her. From what she said, she just had a bad breakup."

"I can relate to that."

"I can too, but to be honest I'm mostly focused on this insanely awesome redhead I've been spending time with recently."

She leaned in and kissed me.

"I'm sure everything will be fine," she said.

"Assuming we survive a night on our own," I whispered as I leaned in and kissed her cheek. She suddenly smiled brightly and she wrapped her arms around my neck.

"I think we'll manage. A whole night on our own sounds like just what we need."

She turned and smacked my ass before disappearing into her studio. I stood there for a long moment in complete and total awe.

I finally decided to take my writing down to the water again, and this time I was not going to get distracted. I was going to start something, and it was going to have meaning. I'd been so lost in memory the whole time I was there, with a few brief pauses in the present, and I was ready to be done. Jane was going to bring more history with her than I could probably handle, and I didn't need it in my writing.

Once again I failed miserably.

I'm sitting at my desk with the final edits of my book, and I can't make heads or tails of it. I've spent far too much time with it for it all to make sense and with each page that I turn I'm more lost than when I started.

I don't pick up my phone when it pings next to me, but I can see out of the corner of my eye that I got a text. It's probably Jane telling me when she'll be home, and I cover it with a sheet of paper so I don't have to think. I need to rewrite and I need to make changes that make sense. I stare at the huge sections that have simply been crossed out and I shudder. I don't know where to begin.

I finally pull my phone out from beneath the pile, even though I haven't started editing. The message is short. It's four words long. It's not something you send in a text.

"I lost the baby."

Chapter Sixteen

The following day was hot. We had a quiet night before, and Stephen and Paul were up and out of the house before I woke up. Even the breeze coming through the window was warm, and Issa and I were both wearing shorts and tee shirts. Sweat clung to my forehead and for much of the day neither one of was inclined to do or say much. It was Issa who finally discovered inspiration.

"So, how do you feel about skinny-dipping?" she asked. "I think it's hot enough for a little afternoon swim. What about you?"

"Are you serious?" I asked her.

She stood up and looked at me daringly. Two seconds later she pulled her shirt off over her head and turned towards the back door. She was wearing nothing beneath it, and I stared at her freckled shoulders as she opened the door and started running down the path towards the water. I ran inside, grabbed two towels from the bathroom and chased her out the door. By the time I arrived on the small beach by the house she was in the water and a small pile of clothes sat on a rock by the shore.

"You coming in?" she yelled.

"Are you really naked?" I called out. Fuck, I couldn't see a thing. This was totally not fair.

"Of course I am! Now come on," she called as she swam out a bit. I pulled off my shirt, and stepped out of my shorts as I watched her red hair bob among the waves. I stood for a moment before finally dropping my boxers and running down into the splashing surf. My heart skipped a few beats as I felt the cold burst through me, but it was just hot enough out that I was glad for the chill. I swam out towards Issa and found her standing on a rock with the water nearly up to her chin. There was room next to her and she wrapped her arms around me until I felt the warmth of her body beneath the waves. The sun was still bright above us and we held each there for a long time before she closed her eyes.

When I kissed her I shivered. Her lips were soft and warm and her breath tasted nothing like wine and everything like Issa. The kiss was gentle and tender, and the longing it brought up was more than just desire. It was a kiss that wanted breakfast and warm sheets; it was a kiss that wanted to hold hands and smile and it was a kiss that wanted to dance naked on the beach and do more of everything. Most of all it was a kiss that I didn't want to end.

As the kiss went on, our warmth began to fade and the cold water pulled the heat from our limbs with unending determination. I wrapped my arms around the small of her back and pulled her tighter to me and she held a hand to my face. I slid my hands down further and pulled her leg up around my waist as we struggled to keep our balance in the bossy waves.

"Let's go inside," she whispered, and we pushed back toward the shore. I wrapped a giant towel around us both as we stood on the rocky strand. She shivered as our cold bodies touched, but we kissed again and it didn't matter.

We tied the towels around us and carried our clothes back up to the house. She didn't stop as she headed towards her bedroom, and I paused in the hallway, not sure what to do. She turned to me and beckoned with one finger. I closed the door behind me, and when I turned around she was standing naked in front of me. The curtains were closed and the room was dark, but I could see her body clearly, and she looked nervous as she clasped her hands in front of her.

I let my own towel fall to the floor as I walked toward her. She kissed me as we backed up to the bed and her hands were now warm as she explored my body. She sat down and looked up at me as she pressed her palms against my stomach and slid them up to my chest.

"This time I'm going to make you come. A lot."

"Issa, I don't care what happens at all. All that matters is—"

She shut me up as she knelt and took me into her mouth, but the photo of her and Paul stared at me from the bedside table. The room was unfamiliar and no matter how much I wanted her, my nerves kept kicking me and her adorations had little effect. Before long she pulled me down onto the bed and wrapped her arms around my neck.

"Is everything okay?"

"Everything is amazing," I said before kissing her again. "Maybe I got used to having Sebastien here as well."

"Do you miss him?" she cooed. "Would it make you happier if he was here too? Did you like him watching as you fucked me?"

I kissed her neck and the slopes of her breasts before moving down, taking a nipple between my lips and teeth as she cried out. I ran my hand along her thigh until I found soft red curls beneath my fingertips. She opened to my touch and I slid two fingers inside her as she arched her back to meet me. She moaned loudly, and I pressed even harder. I touched her and kissed her, and each time she moaned her sounds grew deeper and stronger.

"Fuck me," she whispered and suddenly she sounded like someone else. Maybe it was the tone of her voice or the way her body moved, but my mind was full of Jane and I couldn't find my way back. I shook my head and tried to return to the present, but it was useless. When she reached down and found me still soft, I rolled over next to her on the bed and rubbed my eyes. She rolled over and kissed my cheek and rubbed my chest.

"It's okay," she told me as she kissed my neck. "We are not in a hurry tonight at all. In fact, we have the whole night ahead of us, and tomorrow morning as well. There's time for everything."

"I'm just nervous. It's strange to be in your bedroom, and I'm just nervous, I guess. Did I say I was nervous?"

"Shh," she whispered. "Let's take it slowly and do what feels good. We can just lie here and kiss all night if you like, and we can be as quiet as you want."

"I want more, I'm just..."

"It's okay," she said kissing me again. "There will be plenty of time for other things later." She rolled her leg over my thigh, and I felt her breasts press into my chest. I pressed my knee against her and she moaned quietly into my ear as I slid my hand down the small of her back and over the curve of her ass.

I pulled her to me and kissed her slowly and deeply as I silently scolded myself. Why was it so hard to stay where I was?

She was beautiful, and sexy, and I was naked in bed with her. Her touch was strong and gentle, and her hair smelled like salt air and everything else that I loved. I tried to imagine myself inside her, her body writhing beneath me, and still nothing happened. I remembered Sebastien and wondered if a pinch of jealousy would inspire me, but even that failed to help.

"I'm sorry," I whispered in her ear between kisses.

"James, by the time you've reached forty-two you've seen more soft penises than you know what to do with. It's okay. I promise."

"I'm not sure the vast number of cocks you've seen is making me feel better."

She smacked my chest lightly and kissed me again.

"That's not what I meant! I'm just saying it's not the end of the world. In fact, in almost every case, a little bit of patience and a lot of openness leads to wonderful things, and you and I are going to have wonderful things."

"I just feel silly. Ever since our threesome I've wanted you on my own, and now that you're here it just too much. Hell, even before then I wanted you. Since the very first day I arrived, I wanted..."

"Really?" she said, interrupting me. "The very first day? What did you want to do with me?" She was teasing me and I liked the sound of her voice when she did it. She sounded just like Issa, not like Jane at all.

"Mostly I wanted to see what was under that dress."

She rolled over on top of me and sat up in the dimming light, pulling her hair back.

"So, what do you think?" she asked.

"I think you're the prettiest thing I've ever seen."

"Woman, James. I'm the prettiest woman you've ever seen," and then she was against me, kissing me as she laughed, and I held her to me and tried not to cry.

We kissed for hours that night, but despite our best efforts, sex was not in the cards. I touched her and kissed her, and I pushed my memories as deeply into my mind as they could go. She came for me with soft whispers in my ears and she held me until neither of us could keep our eyes open.

When I finally slept, I fell into a night full of dreams that didn't want to be one thing. Hair changed from black to red and the streets of New York rolled down to the open ocean. There was a baby crying and a gull singing, but none of it stayed with me when I woke up. All it did was leave an empty space in my stomach.

Issa woke me with a kiss. It was soft and gentle and my dreams vanished as her hair brushed my cheek.

"Last night was wonderful," she said as she rolled over on top of me. I was slowly waking up, and she had opened the window to let in a cool breeze. Sitting on the table next to the bed was a hot cup of coffee.

"Despite...?" I asked as I reached over and took a sip.

"Everything was perfect. It was sweet, and sexy, and your body felt so good next to mine. I could have slept all day."

I drank my coffee and tried to feel as excited about it as she did. I felt ridiculous, and pathetic, and I couldn't believe she was actually as happy as she looked to be. Issa interrupted my thoughts by kissing me on the mouth once more. She crawled on top of me and I wrapped my arms around her.

"I promise it was perfect. You've fucked me once, and I promise that you will again."

The boat arrived at six o'clock that evening and the three of them stood on deck all in a row. Jane looked like New York as she stepped off the boat, and I was instantly homesick—with an emphasis on sick. Her black jacket and skirt neatly matched her hair and her luggage matched her purse. Stephen took her bag and rolled it up the dock.

Rather than immediately head out to the house we decided to sit and have a drink at the café. It was a surreal experience.

I expected Jane to order a glass of wine or a scotch, but instead she asked for a Geary's Summer Ale. I looked at her with a hint of confusion.

"I'm drinking local. Besides, it's fucking summer."

Paul ordered another ale, so Issa and I did the same. Stephen got an iced coffee.

"It's summer now," I told her. "But you just missed a week of rain and cold. You must have brought the sun."

She ignored me and turned to Stephen.

"So, what's a handsome kid like you doing on an island like this?"

"You know, keeping away from the drugs and hoes on the mainland," he answered with a grin.

"Sounds like a great plan. All I can say is that I am so fucking happy to be here I can't even tell you. New York is so goddamn hot right now that I've been walking around my apartment naked for a week, even with the air conditioner on. Have you ever been to the East Village in July? It's hot as balls, and I don't mean that in a disrespectful way. Or a good way, really. I just mean it's hot."

"James, you failed to mention that she swears like a sailor," Paul said.

"I blame the ferry," she said quickly. "All those husky sailor lads must have corrupted my brain. Either that or this clean air has killed my internal censor. Either way, I'll try to tone it down. I would hate to fucking bother anyone."

This was the Jane I remembered, times ten. She was crass and funny, and she was friendly to ever single person she met, even if it was in her own way. She talked and she listened, asking Stephen questions that had simply never occurred to me. Every time she opened her mouth I braced myself for what might come out, and I realized that she probably did the same with me.

We sat at the café for an hour before we headed back to the house, where we gave her a brief tour before making our way out to the porch.

"This is amazing," Jane said. "I can't believe you get to sit here and watch the ocean all day. I don't know if I could fucking handle it." She sat down and stared out the window at the rocky hills. I looked over at Issa and shrugged. I felt like I had unleashed a storm on our calm seas.

After a moment Jane went back inside and grabbed a bottle of Pappy Van Winkle that she presented to Paul and Issa. Her gratitude was sincere and I could see the tension leaving her body as she settled back onto the couch. It was exactly the same thing I had felt when I first arrived and it was amazing to see it in someone else. Her toes unclenched and she kicked off her shoes.

She slowly stopped tapping her fingers and twirling her hair, and by the time Paul poured us all a glass of the bourbon I could see it in her face.

"If you'd like, you're welcome to sleep out here," Paul offered.

"Are you serious? That would be fucking awesome. I can't remember the last time I slept to the sound of waves and wind, or really anything other than the noise of the bar below my apartment. Damn."

"Where are you living now?" I asked after a moment's silence. It had been a while since we had talked, and I suddenly realized how much I didn't know about Jane's life.

"I'm on the Lower East Side near Ludlow and Stanton. I got a one bedroom walk-up and for the first time in ages I live by myself."

"I've never lived by myself," Issa said.

We all looked at her, but she didn't seem inclined to follow up with anything. She said it with an air of whimsy and something that almost sounded like regret. Paul reached out and took her hand and she leaned up against his shoulder.

"It's been amazing," Jane continued. "I get up when I have to, eat breakfast on my way to work, and my evenings are completely up to me. I can stay home and do nothing, party till the next morning, or invite someone over and sit on the fire escape and watch the people go by on the street.

"When I first moved to New York I lived with my old college roommate and we had a great fucking time. But it was parties and late nights and there was no such thing as quiet or solitude. A few years later I moved in with James and—"

"We all know how that ended," I said.

"That's not what I meant," she said quietly. "I just mean that living alone isn't something I've done before, and I didn't realize how much I'd enjoy it. Even in school I had roommates and at home there were always my sisters. I never realized that I like to be alone sometimes."

We were all quiet for a few solid minutes, and the breeze outside the window picked up. The sound was pleasing and the cool air on my face felt amazing. Jane sat next to me on the couch looking eager and hopeful, but I was completely unsure what I or the island could offer her. My life was moving along better than I had ever hoped, and suddenly she was there with more expectations than I could handle.

Later that evening I took her for a walk down to the water. Rumor had gotten around to her about what I was doing, and she was full of questions that I didn't want to answer. As we walked out the back door I found myself looking longingly at Issa and wishing we could vanish on our own. Her face was turned to Paul and as hard as I tried I couldn't catch her eye.

"So, are you really burning shit? I mean, not to sound like a bitch, but that's a completely fucking insane thing to do."

"How about, 'Wow, James, I'm so glad that you're writing again'?"

"You're not writing again. You're putting things down on paper and you're burning it. It's art. Or possibly a symptom of depression. Whatever it is, it worries me."

I stopped at the end of the trail and looked out over the water. Jane sat down on a flat rock and didn't stop shaking her head. It was cool and the sun was nearly gone. The sky was a brilliant orange and we could just barely see the last glimmer of light as it vanished over the mainland.

"Jane, why are you here?"

"It's good to see you too."

"I'm serious. I haven't heard from you in six months, and you write to me out of the blue. We haven't written letters since they were dirty ones, and now this. I mean, what is this supposed to be? An intervention? Because I think I'm doing fine."

"You really cut right to the chase, huh? Maybe I just missed you and wanted to see you again. Maybe it really was a shitty breakup, and I needed a vacation. Why did you invite me if you didn't want me here?"

"It's not that I don't want you. I just don't know what you're doing. And when you need a vacation you go to Berlin or Amsterdam. You don't come to the middle of nowhere Maine."

She leaned forward on her hands and looked out over the water just as the last light faded away. There were lines on her face I didn't remember, and her hair was longer than the last time I'd seen her. I had a million questions, and none of them were things I wanted to ask.

"Suzanne told me not to come."

"I haven't talked to her at all. Other than one postcard."

"She said you found someone."

"Can we stick with you for a minute? Look, I'm happy to see you, and I think you'll love it here. Issa and Paul are amazing, and Stephen is a cool kid. The island is great, but I still don't understand."

She leaned down on her hands and rubbed the sides of her face. Jane wasn't patient, but she knew how to make me wait for something.

"Mark left me. He said he was trying, but that I wasn't. He told me that I was still dating you in my head and he wasn't going to compete with someone who wasn't even there. He told me to figure my shit out before I bother trying again."

"Jane, what happened with us was..."

"Too much. I told him that. I said there was no way back from any of it, but he didn't care. So I came here."

"And what am I supposed to do? Forget everything that happened? Forget the book and the lying? Do you want me to just pretend none of that stuff happened, and try to give it another shot?"

"You're seeing someone. I can tell by the way you talk."

"It's complicated."

"It's always complicated with you. You get yourself wrapped

up into things you don't understand, and you don't think at all. You just go with the flow regardless of the consequences and things fall apart around you. Tell me you're not sleeping with the married lady."

"I said it was complicated."

"What the fuck, James? Does Paul know?"

"Of course he does. They have an open marriage."

"Jesus Christ, do you think you could have put some of this in the letter? Oh by the way, I'm dating the married woman I'm staying with who just happens to be polyamorous or a swinger or something. Come on up, we're having an orgy this weekend."

"It's not like that at all. They're just open people."

"And what are you going to do when you fall madly in love with her? Because you know that you will. You'll fall head over heels and suddenly sharing her with someone, even someone as nice as that Paul guy, is going to feel like a whole mess of hurt. Talk about a set up."

"You really want to just piss on my parade here, don't you. I'm fucking writing again, I'm having a great time, I'm hooking up with an amazing woman—who is completely stable, by the way—and you have to show up and tear it all apart. Maybe I shouldn't have written that fucking letter."

"Because it's still all about your writing."

"You know, it's nice to see that after all this time we still can yell at each other like pros. We're standing on the beach after one of the most glorious sunsets I've ever seen, and we're yelling at each other like fucking children. No wonder we worked out so well."

Jane stood and picked up a stone in the dark. She skipped it out into the waves before bending down and picking up another. It followed the first into the cold water before she turned to me. I wasn't sure whether I wanted to take her into my arms or run back to the house on my own. Nothing felt like a good choice.

"I'm sorry," she finally whispered. "I didn't know what else to do, James. I'm so fucking sorry."

She was in my arms without another word and her tears destroyed every barricade I had. I held her tightly and kissed the top of her head as she sobbed onto my shoulder. Her whole body shook as she cried, and somehow I managed to forget everything else. I let it all go except for the wonderful and familiar feeling of her body against mine.

Chapter Eighteen

Finding time with Issa was suddenly impossible. I was immediately a tour guide and a host, and I didn't know how to stop. Jane and I ignored the night before as we had always been so good at doing, and we played a game that was familiar. I took her to the café in the morning and introduced her to Abigail. We sat and drank coffee and she filled me in on her life. We talked and we chatted and if you saw us together you might think we were simply old friends.

When she talked about Mark it was painfully free of his accusations. He was a lawyer who worked downtown and they met through a mutual friend with good taste in bars. They flirted shamelessly a few nights in a row before he took her home, and before either of them knew what was happening they were a couple. They had dinners together and introductions to their friends. They went to art exhibits and drank cocktails on the roof of the Museum. They slipped into coupledom without so much as a thought, and she thought they were happy.

When she delved into their sex life, which sounded as seamless and easy as everything else, I found myself mostly at ease and even slightly engaged. I laughed when she told me his quirks and habits, and even the gory details didn't bother me. I was sincerely interested. She told me of sex on his rooftop deck, and slipping into the bathroom of the Campbell Apartment for a quickie. She said it all with a smile of warm recollection, but underneath it all was a question.

Two nights after Jane arrived I walked out onto the porch to find her smoking a cigarette with Paul, and they paused just long enough when I opened the door that I raised an eyebrow. They were sitting across from each other smoking, drinking wine, and laughing, and I tried hard not to make any assumptions.

"Would you rather drink nothing but wine for the rest of your life, or never fucking drink wine again?" Jane asked as I sat down next to Paul on the couch.

"Nothing at all? No water, no beer, no nothing but wine?"

"That's the rule," Paul said.

"Fuck, I think I could do it with beer, but I don't know about wine. I mean, beer for breakfast is one thing, but wine?"

"How about a champagne cocktail?" Jane asked with a slur.

"No!" Paul interrupted. "It's wine or nothing. No orange, peach, or pear juice for brunch, and no seltzer and lemon for a spritzer. That's the rule and I'd do it in a heartbeat. I mean, if I had to make the choice."

"I could do it too," Jane said, and it was clear that she had in fact been drinking nothing but wine for a few hours by then. "I mean, especially if I could be sitting on this fucking porch, talking to two handsome men, and watching the waves go by."

This was starting to feel way too familiar.

"Come in," Paul told her.

"Come in where?"

"Watching the waves come in, not go by. The waves don't go by. Boats go by, and muskrats go by, but the waves come in, and I could watch the waves come in with you all day."

"Oh, fuck your semantics. I'll watch the wave do whatever I want."

In the spirit of catching up with them, I opened another bottle of red, poured myself a big glass, and looked out over the water. They were both lost as I watched the waves crash against the rocks, and I wondered where Issa was. Since Jane's arrival she had mostly stayed in her studio, and there were times when I thought she might be avoiding me.

"Do you know where your wife is?" I finally asked.

"She's in her studio. She's been going crazy on a new project, and I can hardly get her out. I even opened her favorite bottle, but she doesn't want to leave."

"Maybe I'll see if I can entice her out," I said, but still I didn't move.

Jane was lost in thought each time I looked at her, and half of the time she simply smiled in the general direction of Paul. She did glance at me on occasion, and she threw me a tipsy wink when she had her glass in hand, but she was clearly focused on one thing.

As the night wore on and I started to get tired, neither one of them looked interested in moving. Stephen was reading in the living room, and Issa had never appeared. I finally gave in and left them there. I could hear them laughing as I walked down the hall, and as much as I tried to push it out of my mind it always slipped back in. There was a long pause after my knock on the door to Issa's studio.

"Who is it?" she finally said.

"It's James."

The door opened slowly and she let me in before closing it behind us. The room was a mess, but she had clearly been working. There was clay on the wheel and more tools than I could name lined her bench. She had drawings on the table, and stacks of glaze covered the chair.

"What's up?" she asked.

"Am I bothering you? I missed you and I wanted to see how you were doing."

She sat down on the small loveseat in the corner. It was

covered with an old sheet and I had never once seen her sitting on it. We could hear Jane and Paul through the wall, though their voices were muffled by the wind outside.

"Come sit."

I did as I was told without question, but I paused before reaching out for her. We had been so close to something the day before Jane arrived, and suddenly it had vanished in a blink.

"Is everything okay?" I asked.

"I've been hiding, haven't I."

I nodded.

"I do that sometimes when I'm not sure how to behave. I don't know, James. I'm not trying to be weird, but I don't know what to do with her. I don't want to be rude, but at the same time I miss you too, and every time you walk by I just want to reach out and take your hand."

"Why don't you? I told Jane the first night she arrived that you and I have a relationship. Of some sort."

"I'm sure that clarified things."

I leaned back, but when I looked at her again she was laughing and it was the most welcome sight in the world. She leaned over and kissed me before taking my hand in hers.

"I don't know why I feel weird. She just knows you so well. Every time she says something that I didn't know I get jealous. It's silly, right? I'm supposed to be an expert at this. It's not just that though. Paul has been flirting with her as well, and she's great. She's smart and sarcastic and sometimes I feel like I can't keep up. I feel old and slow around her."

"Issa, I can't begin to tell you how much I've missed you. Jane is..."

"What is she?"

"She's challenging. She brought a whole lot of memories with her and she doesn't even realize it. I'm not sure what to do with her. But you are gorgeous and sexy, and if I don't get to spend another night with you soon I'm going to lose my mind."

"Another night sounds like a dream to me."

One kiss led to another on the tiny couch, but we were gentle and kind rather than passionate. We touched each other's arms and kissed chins and noses. A few brushes of breasts and thighs brought moans to our lips, but mostly we held each other for long silent moments, and nearly fell asleep wrapped in each other's arms. When we finally said goodnight it was with a promise. We'd find time one way or another.

I lay in bed for over an hour. I tried to start writing three or four times, but ever since Jane's arrival it had been nearly impossible. My hand wouldn't move. She was too close to everything for me to write about her, but there was no room for anything else. I stood up and opened the window. I paced back and forth and I tried to touch my toes. I closed the window and turned on the light. I looked through my written memory of my morning with Issa and Sebastien, but even that failed to inspire me. I couldn't sleep, I couldn't relax, and I couldn't even get myself off.

At three in the morning, Jane slipped into bed with me. She was quiet and even though I was groggy, I could tell that something was wrong. I turned on the light and she leaned in and buried her head against my shoulder.

"What is it?" I asked as I pulled her to me. She looked miserable, but I didn't want to force the question. She was wearing just a tee shirt and underwear, and her hair was a mess. Finally she looked up at me.

"You're going to hate me," she said quietly.

"What happened?" I asked.

"I slept with Paul."

"What?" I said, louder than I intended. "You mean, just now?"

"Yes," was all she said as she pulled me close again and wrapped her arms around me. I was still confused, but I found myself less surprised than expected. What I didn't understand was why she was there. Why was she in my bed, and why was this suddenly my problem?

"Was it fun?" I finally asked.

"Yes," she said with a pouty face and a wrinkled nose.

"Was it safe?" I asked again.

"Yes," she answered, this time with a hint of pride.

"Do you like him?" I asked, not sure if I wanted to hear the answer, but convinced I was doing the right thing.

"I do like him, but I feel like I fucked up. I mean, I don't really know him at all, and I thought…"

"What did you think?"

"I thought you and I might be trying to make something happen again."

It was my turn to sit up in bed and stare at her.

"Are you saying you want to get back together with me? After everything that happened and…"

"No. I don't know. Fuck, James, this is confusing. I thought I would come up here and it would sort itself out. We've had time and distance and we've both said we're sorry. I guess I thought it was worth a try."

"Last time we talked you told me you didn't miss that relationship at all."

"I don't. I don't want that relationship. I don't know what I want, but you seem to be working something out. Paul is so fucking charming and when he explained their situation— granted, it was after two bottles of wine—it just made sense. It sounded smart and sophisticated, and I figured if you could do it, then so could I."

"Issa and I have barely even slept together. We haven't even had sex other than the threesome, but…"

"Wait. What? You had a fucking threesome? With her and Paul? Why is this the first time I'm hearing about this?"

"It wasn't with Paul. I told you it was complicated."

"Yes, and I thought dating a married woman counted as complicated. I didn't expect it to be a group sex type of complicated. This is far more interesting. And possibly hot. You know I have a threesome thing."

"We started flirting the day I got here, but nothing happened until a week ago. There was a guy staying in town and we invited him out to dinner. One thing led to another and..."

"And you had yourself a nice little threesome with a married woman and a tourist."

"That's about the short of it. What's wrong with that?" It was my turn to look smug, and the expression of shock on her face was worth everything. She shook her head as she looked at me, and I wasn't sure if she even believed me.

"All I'm saying is that you just got here and now suddenly you're fucking someone on the porch. I love the porch. I want to fuck on the porch."

"It was only a little sex."

"What does that mean?"

"I mean, it was like quick sex. We were drunk and exhausted and it was super awkward and sweet. We kissed and groped, and I didn't even take off my shirt. The actual sex part lasted for about three minutes."

"And now you're in my bed."

"I got lonely. And I miss sleeping with you."

"You're still drunk."

"And you're still handsome."

I was tempted to kiss her and pull her closer, but I was sure she wasn't ready for another round of sex, especially with another man. I also wasn't sure I could. I loved her, and part of me even wanted her, but Issa was so much in my mind it was nearly impossible to let go. I remembered for a moment that Issa had gone from me and Sebastien to Paul in the same amount of time, but it was all too much.

It was Jane who finally spoke.

"Do you think you could do it?"

"Live on an island and drink wine by the case?"

"Don't be a dick. I mean, do you think you could have more than one girlfriend?"

It took me a long time to say anything; every fear I had popped into my mind at once, and I tried to settle them. Did I really want someone who wanted other people? I didn't want to leave things so open that I could never feel safe, and yet Paul and Issa were two of the calmest people I knew. I thought of Issa and Sebastien and felt my stomach twitch. I thought of Jane and Paul and it continued, but when I remember Paul and Issa sitting together on the couch after that first night apart I saw a glimmer of possibility.

"I don't know," was my answer. "A week ago it would have been no, but now I just don't know. Issa is amazing, and I'm not jealous of Paul at all. I keep thinking that they're crazy, and then remember that I'm doing it too. At least to a certain extent. But I don't know about everything else. We've hardly talked about what it all means and where it's going."

"Maybe we don't have to figure anything out tonight. But if you let me sleep here I promise I'll be here in the morning. I'll make the coffee, and we can talk about anything you like."

I kissed her lips softly and she returned it with a gentleness that surprised me. She whispered she loved me into my ear before reaching over and turning off the light. I pulled the blanket up over us and closed my eyes. Despite all the confusion, all the jealously, and all the fear, it felt good to have a warm body next to mine, and after hours of tossing and turning I finally slept.

Chapter Nineteen

I left Jane in bed the next morning and walked down to the sea on my own. A blue cotton sweater wrapped around my body like a blanket. The wind was cold and crisp, and I wanted to stare out over the water and never leave.

When I opened my notebook I came face to face with the last words I had written. I bit my lip and tried not to read them again. Jane was sleeping only a few hundred yards away, and here I was, standing by the water holding on to memories I had struggled to forget. I sat down on the rocks and braced my body and my mind. There are some things that you can't put off.

"Is this what you think of me?" she asks.

"I don't understand." Talk about an understatement. I can write whole books on what I don't understand. In fact, often I think that I have.

"This woman in the book. This girl. This insecure, neurotic, possessive bitch, is supposed to be me?"

"It's a novel, Jane. No one is supposed to be you."

"You hate her and destroy her without even thinking about how I might feel. You build her up, and then suddenly in the middle of it all, you just cut her open."

Now I'm confused. I'm desperately trying to remember what happened and how it all changed, but it doesn't make sense. My Jean was wonderful, and even if she was a little extreme, none of those things sounded right.

"*Jane, what are you talking about? I love that character.*"

"*You said that you would rather drown than have our baby.*"

She's crying and shaking and suddenly it hits me. Somehow she read words never meant to go anywhere. She read an outburst of anger, fear, and intoxication that was cut before my editor even saw it. There was only one scene she could be talking about, and I deleted it before it ever saw the light of day. Clearly that wasn't soon enough.

I look at her with confusion but she's not paying me any attention. I can feel my anger getting the best of me.

"*Jane, that's not in the book. I didn't leave that in the book. When did you read that? Why would you read that?*"

And her crying is worse than before, and I can barely stand it. I want to make it go away, and I want to hide from it. It's mixed in with my own fear and frustration and suddenly I have an awful thought that I can't get rid of.

"*When did you read that?*" *I ask her. I'm trying to be gentle, but I have to know. My world is changing around me. "*When did you read that?*"*

"*Oh God, James, I'm so sorry.*"

She can't say anything else, and I don't know what to do. I want to hold her and yell at her at the same time. I don't know what she did, but my guessing is tearing me open. For some reason I can't let go.

"*Jane, did you do something? Did you do something after reading that passage?*"

She looks up at me with bright red eyes and she shakes her head back and forth as she crosses her arms and begins to walk away. She's picking up her things and she won't answer me. No matter how I ask her, she's not saying a word and I'm beginning to lose myself.

"*Please, Jane. Please tell me no.*"

She's at the door with a bag and she hasn't stopped crying. I try to reach out but she brushes my hand away and won't let me touch her.

"I thought you didn't want her. I'm so sorry. I thought you didn't want her."

As the door closes behind her, my own tears finally burst through my anger.

"I didn't know it was a girl," I whisper as I fall to my knees by the door.

How do you mourn hope? On the edge between insurmountable and never ending, can you weigh suffering and pick and choose what you carry on your own? I wouldn't have chosen this. That much I know.

I didn't even bother to tear the pages from the notebook. All I knew at that moment was that I might need them again. I might need to remember the sorrow I felt that afternoon, before it was replaced by rage.

I turned to find Paul standing behind me on the shore and I nearly jumped from the surprise. He was wearing drawstring pants and a sweatshirt that looked as old as the house behind him. I waved at him and he stumbled down over the rocks to where I was standing. He sat down and cracked his knuckles in front of him with a wide yawn.

"Do you come down here every morning? I've lived here for eight years, and I think I've come down here less than a dozen times. I really need to get my priorities straightened out."

"I don't think I'll ever get used to it. It makes me feel small."

I sat down next to him and I wondered whether he was going to say anything about the night before. I didn't even know whether I wanted him to or not.

"What are you writing about?" he asked instead.

"Jane," I said without thinking. "How can one woman make my mind do so many things?"

"She's rather compelling. I saw she was sleeping in your room when I came out. Did she..."

"She told me."

"Ah. I thought she might. She sounded very sincere in her desire to 'do this properly,' as she said."

"I've been writing about her too much. I came up here to escape those memories and yet every day they come pouring back in. I keep trying to distract myself and I've tried over and over again to write other things. I've managed it a few times, but even then it's mixed up with everything else. Even with Issa and Sebastien I could barely manage to stay in the present."

"You would think that when the present is a good place to be that it would get easier. But it never is. In fact, the best times are some of the hardest for me."

"I wrote something once that she should never had read."

"In your book?"

"No, it was while I was writing the book though. I was scared one night and I let myself go. I needed to vent and the only way I know how to do that is with my writing. So, I put down things and somehow she found them. She found them and she thought they were true."

"That sounds complicated."

"How do you forgive someone when you think it may all be your fault?"

Paul closed his eyes for a while and I wasn't sure if he was thinking or ignoring me. I looked back at the waves and figured maybe the question didn't have an answer.

"I suspect you have to forgive yourself first," he finally said.

We didn't talk much as we wound our way back up to the house, and everyone else was still sleeping as we went in to fix coffee. He measured the coffee precisely and he poured the water slowly. We leaned on the counter as the smell began to fill the room and I held my mug to my chest in anticipation. It was one of Issa's and it was the same color as the walls. It was nice to have Paul there next to me, and even when I pictured him and Jane wrapped up in each other's arms I felt more comfort from him than anything else.

"I have a logistics question for you," Paul said, breaking our silence.

"Not my forte, but go for it."

"I don't want this to come out the wrong way, but what do you think about asking Jane to rent the room above the café? I don't want to be unwelcoming, and we love having her here, but between the four of us there are about ten different relationships, and a little space might give us all some room to breathe.

"I haven't mentioned it to her, and I don't want to insult her—especially after last night—but in the end it will make some things easier. I have no idea if that was a fluke or not, but having an extra room for play time might make everyone happier. If you know what I mean."

"So, we'll rent the room about the café. For sex."

"Yeah. Basically. That's about what I was thinking. Too soon?"

"No, I don't think it's too soon. I had good sex up there."

"Oh right. When you were fucking my wife and that French dude. I think I heard about that. I'm sure you got a good look around. Is it nice?"

"I especially loved the ceiling paint," I said, and Paul and I struggled not to laugh too loudly. I hadn't realized how much I had been keeping inside me until we started to joke about it, and it all came out at once.

"I don't mean to be crass, I just like saying that on occasion. The fucking my wife bit, I mean. It makes me feel cool."

"You're super cool, Paul. Definitely one of the coolest guys on the island. Next to me, of course."

"Obviously. So, what do you think? Would it be too much of a financial issue? I don't know anything about Jane when it comes to that. I don't think Abigail charges much, though."

"It's worth asking."

The five of us ate breakfast on the porch, and before I could say a thing Paul brought up the question.

"Did I really fuck things up?" Jane suddenly asked. "I know I'm the new person here, and you didn't really invite me up, and now I feel like I've totally messed up your little arrangement."

I looked at Paul, but before either of us could speak Issa jumped in.

"My husband is just hoping to get you alone. Again."

"I, um..."

"I'm kidding, Jane. Well, sort of. The point is that we like having you here. And honestly, it doesn't really matter who stays there. It's complicated out here with all of us, and having a room to play in where we don't have to worry about noise could be fun for all of us."

"You mean it's complicated out here with me." We all looked at Stephen and I was at a complete loss for words. I didn't have a single idea about how to work him into this conversation.

"Stephen, I mean it's complicated in general. But yes. You're a part of this family too and you get a say in what happens. Especially when it affects your home. We invited James and Jane without so much as asking how you felt about it, and I'm sorry for that. But now you're a part of the conversation."

"Great. Just the conversation I want to have on a summer morning." He looked down into his coffee and it was Jane who broke the silence.

"A week ago, I thought I was open minded. I live in New York, I have a cool job at a design agency and I once lived with a stripper for almost a year. But you guys put a new meaning to the word."

"It comes with old age," Paul said. "Once you get to be my age, there's not much point in mincing words."

"James?" Jane asked, looking over at me. She didn't have to say more than that for me to know every question in her mind. Did I want her to go? Was it okay if she started sleeping with

Paul? Was she really going to stay on the island long enough for it to matter?

"I think it's a good idea," I said.

"Is that the place Sebastien was living in?" Stephen asked. Issa nodded, but didn't say a thing. "How about I live there, and you all can have your crazy grown-up time here at the house without me. Do they have cable?"

"Stephen we're not throwing you out of the house. We're just trying to take some of the pressure off everyone being under one roof."

"So, my options are to say yes, Jane should move out, or no, she should stay here? I'm so glad I get a choice in this."

"Stephen..."

"Why do you even bother including me in these conversations?" He was up and in the house before anyone could say a thing and Paul was right behind him. I heard a door slam, someone yell, and then all was quiet again.

"Well, that worked out well. Anyone want another cup of coffee?" Issa was trying to fake a smile, and while it didn't work especially well I appreciated the effort.

"It really is a simple life up here isn't it?"

"Jane, it's not normally this crazy, but..."

"I was joking James."

We sat in silence for what felt like a very long time. Issa got up and poured us all another cup, and there were a few moments where looking out over the water did in fact feel calming. I nearly opened my mouth three or four times, but there was nothing to say. About twenty minutes later Paul came back and sat down.

"He's fine. He's just frustrated by the whole thing and doesn't especially want to be a part of our discussions when it comes to the logistics of hooking up."

"I can understand that." And it was true. After spending an afternoon in a cave with Stephen I didn't really want to be a part of it either. And I was right in the middle of it all.

"I just wanted him to be included. He does live here and he does get a say in what happens, but maybe this wasn't the right way to do it." Paul stared into his mug for a moment before looking up again with a grin. "On the other hand, I think he'd be happier here if he had some of his space back. So, no matter who is spending what night where, I think the apartment is a good idea. Issa?"

"I'm in."

And so, it was settled. Just like that. Paul and Jane decided to ride into town and talk with Abigail, and before Issa or I said another thing they were gone. We stood outside the house watching them ride off down the path and it was a strange feeling. I could still hear their laughter, and for a moment I didn't recognize her. There was nothing of New York left at all.

"That was quick."

"You mean them two?" I asked. She nodded.

"Should I be worried about them? I think she's a nice girl, but..."

"But it was quick."

I walked Issa into her studio, and I kissed her for a long time against the door.

"We have a habit of this."

"Of what?" I asked.

"Of kissing like this until I'm so frustrated I need to do something about it. Now are you going to come in here and fuck me or am I going to have to take care of it myself?"

"What about Stephen?" I asked.

"He went out the back while we sending them into town. We have time. And an empty house."

I closed the door behind us without another word.

We stumbled back out later to the sounds of voices in the

living room. Jane and Paul were laughing and they looked like teenagers caught in a park when we opened the door.

"She was happy to give me the room," Jane said with a laugh she tried to cut short.

"And it looks like you might have had a tour?" Issa raised her eyebrow in question.

"I wouldn't say a tour, but we wanted to break it in a bit." Paul looked slightly sheepish, but he wasn't hiding a thing. Issa frowned at him. "What? We didn't stay for too long, but it's a great spot. As you two know."

"I didn't say anything. I mean, it's not like James and I have a leg to stand on." It was Issa's turn to look sheepish.

"When are you moving in?" I asked.

"You in a hurry?"

"Jane, that's not what I meant. I'm just curious."

Paul stepped behind her, and before we could say another word he and Issa opened the door to the porch and left us alone.

"You're still angry with me. Maybe I should just go back to New York."

"Jane, look, just sit down for a minute."

I stood in front of her and realized that wasn't going to work at all. I sat in the big chair and felt small and foolish, but it didn't matter. No matter where I was, we were going to miss each other. We talked past one another and we didn't listen. We opened our mouths before we had time to think, and we had been together just long enough to think we knew something.

"I'm sitting. What?"

"Why are you doing this? You come up here, and within three days you've inserted yourself into my life and there's no way out. You don't just come for a visit. You come and tear everything apart without even thinking. You call me impulsive, but look at you."

"I didn't do a fucking thing, James. I asked you if I could

come. You invited me. And what the fuck do you care who I'm sleeping with? You and Issa are like the little couple that could, and who cares what I do? You've been going through the motions with me, but your eyes never leave her, and even when I'm alone with you it's like she's fucking there."

"Because I'd rather she was! You're driving me crazy, and I can't breathe anymore. I haven't written a goddamn word since you got here, and you haven't even asked. Do you ever think about anyone else?"

"That's rich coming from you. Coming from the guy who has to burn everything he writes because he can't live with it. It's real fucking special. I don't know why I came here either."

"Well, I believe you have somewhere to stay now, don't you."

Jane picked up her bag without another word. She nearly kicked the door open when she walked out, and a minute later I was standing alone in the living room feeling like a complete and total asshole. I walked back to my room, closed the door behind me and climbed into bed without taking off a thing. I lay there staring up at the ceiling, and I didn't leave my room again until the morning.

Chapter Twenty

Issa woke me with a kiss that startled me from my sleep. She pulled back the blanket and crawled into bed next to me. She was wearing her flannel pajamas and they were soft and warm as she pressed her body against me.

"It's cold out," was all she said.

I wrapped my arms around her and kissed her forehead. She rubbed my stomach with one strong hand and nestled down into the crook of my shoulder.

"I don't want to get out of bed."

"It's because you're cranky and probably whiny."

I opened my mouth to disagree but everything that came to mind suddenly sounded cranky. Or whiny. I pulled the sheet up to my chin and snorted.

"See? Cranky."

"I'm angry. There's a difference."

"You sounded more hurt than angry."

"You heard us?"

"James, the whole island heard you. The two of you screamed so loudly Abigail is probably writing an article in the paper about it right now."

"She makes me do crazy things."

"People don't make you do anything. You just respond to her in crazy ways."

"I don't like it when you put it that way."

"It doesn't mean it's not true."

I sighed and sat up in bed. Issa sat up next to me and crossed her legs. Her hair was loose and hung down over her shoulders in a crimson mess. She looked sleepy and brilliant all at once.

"I thought you two were getting along. You convinced me to come out of hiding and you were right. She's lovely. She's kind and funny and if the two of you don't get over whatever shit you're going through it's going to be a very long summer."

"We were going to have a baby."

Issa reached out and took my hand, but again she was silent. What was there to say? It wasn't a question or a request for help. It was just a true thing. We were going to have a baby. And then we weren't.

"Paul and I tried for two years."

"I didn't know that."

"We don't talk about it. Sometimes late at night we say something in passing, but after trying for so long it hurts too much. It's mostly okay, but there are times when I wonder how my life would have been different."

I reached over and pulled her close to me and she climbed into my arms. We lay back down on the bed and she rested her head on my chest. I combed my fingers through her hair. Sometimes I wonder if it's worth it to actually know what you want.

Issa and I slept for an hour before climbing out of bed and making breakfast. Paul was gone, Stephen was sleeping, and the house was quiet. We made scrambled eggs with spinach and Parmesan cheese, and we drank tea instead of coffee. We sat in the kitchen around the counter, and for a few moments it reminded me of my first morning there.

"Are you going to go talk to her? She spent a whole night by herself, and I bet she doesn't feel any better than you do. Paul was going to stop by on his way to work, but he didn't have much time. Also, he's not you."

"What am I going to say?"

"I'm sorry?"

"That's not a good idea. No one likes apologies."

She slapped my arm and pushed me down the hall to the bathroom. She turned on the shower, stripped my clothes off, and pushed me in, and before I knew what was happening she was climbing in behind me. She rubbed soap into my shoulders and she pressed her body against mine until my cock was hard against her skin.

"You are so fucking sexy I can't stand it," I whispered as I kissed her under the falling water.

"And you deserve a treat for being so good." She had that look in her eyes that I longed for every day.

She was on the tile floor seconds later and her mouth was warm and soft. She looked up at me without ever stopping, and between her hands and her lips I had to hold onto the walls to keep from falling. I moaned her name, I closed my eyes, and within minutes I was coming. She laughed as she worked her hands, and when she finally stood and kissed me again the smile wouldn't leave her face.

"Why are you laughing?"

"I've wanted to see you come for weeks."

"I almost came last night in your studio."

"Almost is a big word. But it was worth the wait. The expression on your face was amazing. I think I might love you."

I kissed her again, lifting her off the tiles floor to meet me.

"Say that again," I whispered.

"I love you James. I love you, I love you, I love you."

I knew that I had to go out to the café and I had to see Jane. I had to apologize and I had to do more than that. But first, I had to finish the story. I kissed Issa goodbye on the porch and as much as I didn't want to end it, I finally headed down the path to the water. I found the same spot where I'd sat when I first arrived, and I took out my notebook. I took a deep breath and I began to write. It wasn't my story this time, but it was a story that had to be told.

One night when I'm asleep Jane sits up by herself. Her brain won't stop moving, and she needs to calm her mind. She paces back and forth in the living room and she considers going out for a walk. She pours herself a finger of bourbon and sits in the windowsill.

When she opens my laptop she has no plan at all. Maybe she'll catch up on the news or watch movies until she can sleep, but my novel is open and it's the first time she sees a word. It's been nearly a year since I cut her out completely. With no shoulder to look over, she can't resist what's in front of her.

She skims page after page and she laughs and grins. She likes it and there's a girl named Jean. It is clearly her. She's funny and sarcastic and her dialog is perfect. She scrolls halfway through the text, all of it without thinking, and a paragraph catches her eye. There's something about Jean and it looks important.

Her eyes open as she pours through the words and she begins to shake when she reads it. There's so much anger and fear that she can hardly stomach it. It's written in first person, and it takes Jean apart with a scalpel. I dissect her every thought and I tear open her past. I cuts through her hopes and aspirations with a sarcastic wit that is neither kind nor true. The last sentence on the page makes her heart collapse onto itself.

"If I have to have a baby with this woman I don't think I'll survive. I'll suffocate in her presence, and I'd rather drown than try to swim."

She closes the file and then the laptop. She climbs into bed, but never sleeps. In the morning she doesn't say a word, but on her way to work she calls the clinic to make an appointment.

I stared out over the water for a long time. I didn't bother tearing the pages from my notebook, and my lighter never left my front pocket. I crossed my arms over my chest as I breathed the ocean air and wondered once more what was on the other side. Paul told me one day that the next piece of land off the east coast of the island was Pontevedra in Spain. I wasn't sure if I believed him. It was so far away.

I took one last look before I headed back to the house. I left my notebook by the back door, got on Issa's bicycle, and took a deep breath before starting into town.

I knocked on the door to Jane's apartment as quietly as I could. It took her a while to answer, but when she finally let me in she waved me through to the bed and she sat down. I sat down next to her, and when she looked at me it was so familiar I had to look again. She had been crying, but she was moving through it.

"What do you want? I don't have enough energy left to cry more."

"Can I have a glass of water?"

"The kitchen is over there. Get me one too."

I came back a minute later with two glasses and I sat down on the bed next to Jane. I wanted to tell her it was done. I had finished what I needed to write, and I could start over again, but that wasn't the point. For the first time in over a year I remembered there were two of us. What I could or couldn't do wasn't the only important thing.

"I'm sorry."

"For what?" she asked me.

"For a whole lot of things. To start with, I'm sorry for writing the words that I did, and then I'm sorry for making it all about me. I knew there was more to it, but each time I thought about it all that I knew was you had lied to me. I was angry, but more than anything I was so guilt ridden that I couldn't see past myself. You were never meant to read that. And it was not about you."

I took a deep breath. "She was you. I mean, Jean. The character was you in my mind, and the more I wrote the more I wanted to understand you. I was terrified of what you might think, and one night I got carried away. You had gone out and I didn't know if you were coming home. We had been fighting for days and I did something stupid. I wrote so I could be angry, because I don't know how else to do it. But those words were something else. They weren't fit for human consumption. They were a disaster, but most of all, they were untrue."

She looked at me with open eyes, and the relief I expected didn't come. I thought my words would take away some of the hurt and it would get easier. But with each thing I said she looked more and more miserable.

"I never wanted a baby," she said.

It took everything I had not to respond. I did take her hand in mine, and I did turn to her with as much warmth as I had, but I didn't ask for more. If I had leaned anything from Paul and Issa it was that people need to move in their own time.

"It wasn't you," she said finally. "And it wasn't us. I just don't want children. I was terrified when I found out, and you were so excited that I froze. I spent weeks convincing myself that it was the right thing to do. It was the adult thing to do. It made all the sense in the world, but each time I followed the thought through to the end I woke up in a sweat."

"You could have told me."

"Obviously I couldn't. I mean, yes, it's easy to say that now, but at the time I was paralyzed. I tried and I tried, and when I read that line in your book it was over. It was the out I needed, and I took it."

"And then?"

"And then I fucking lied to you. I lied to you because I didn't want to admit that I had read your work. I lied to you because I was horrified that I had done it without telling you, and I lied to you because in the end, I thought it would be better. I thought it would be easier. I can't handle your unhappiness."

Jane reached over to her purse and pulled out a cigarette. I pulled the Zippo from my pocket and lit it without saying a word. She sat there staring out at the water, and I closed my eyes.

"I can't believe how far away we are," she said between drags. "And even up here, even so damn far from New York, we're still struggling."

"On the bright side, we're good at struggling."

She smoked less than half the cigarette before crushing it out. She turned with a shy grin.

"Do you still like the taste?" she asked.

Our kiss was tender and chaste, but for the briefest of seconds our whole life came back in a tumble. She tasted just like herself, and I remembered a thousand kisses at once. When she pulled away, neither one of us reached out for more. One step at a time.

"Do you love her?" she asked.

"I do."

"Do you love me too?"

"Of course."

"All year I thought that you hated me. After what I did, I would have hated. Suzanne used to tell me you missed me, but I never believed her. I wanted to, but I always remembered you yelling at me when I was leaving. It was the moment I realized you knew what I had done and I couldn't live with it."

"I never hated you. I was angry and I was sad, but I never hated you. I saved that for myself most of the time. I still can't believe I wrote what I did."

"You know that you didn't make me do anything, right? I mean, it was terrible to read, but I was the one who made the decision."

"I know that up here, but not always here," I said, placing

my hand over my heart. "And in some ways it doesn't matter. We should never have let ourselves get that far."

Jane and I sat for a long time looking out at the bay. The room was small and the windows rattled in the wind. She was right: we were so far away from New York that it felt like a different world. When I put my arm around her she collapsed into me and we didn't need words. We had explained everything enough.

It was late in the afternoon by the time we returned to the house.

When Paul got home, he was visibly relieved to see the four of us sitting on the porch. Stephen was telling us about his latest band crush, and Jane and Issa sat next to each other on the couch with almost a touch of familiarity. Paul sat down next to me and raised an eyebrow in question. I just smiled and shrugged.

"Oh, by the way, how do I get my ferry ticket back to the mainland?"

"You buy them at the dock," Issa told her. "Are you going home already?"

"I only have a week off. And as much as I like it up here, some of us have to go back to work."

"You just rented the room, though."

"For four nights. It's Thursday and I'm leaving on Sunday."

Paul looked at me, but once again I didn't have anything to offer. It was the first I was hearing of it. Jane was good at planning ahead; she just wasn't good at letting anyone know.

"Do you have to leave Sunday or can you stay until Monday?"

"I think Sunday. I can technically miss another day, but I'm already going back to a shitstorm, and I don't need to make it any worse."

"Well then, we better get in our fun before you have to go."

"Dad, there are kids here, remember?"

"I was talking about sailing, Stephen."

"Are you serious? I haven't gone sailing since I was a kid. Do you have a boat?" Jane was suddenly more alert than I had seen her all day.

"I've been talking with a friend in town, and he offered to let us borrow his tomorrow. If we're up for it."

"I'm totally in," Stephen exclaimed. "We haven't gone sailing since last summer when Liz—" He stopped.

"It's okay," Issa said. "You can say her name."

"Since Liz was here," he finished.

"Well, I'm in," I said. "I haven't been off the island since I got here, and I haven't been sailing since... well, never." I looked over at Jane. "At least we'll get more time together before you leave."

"Oh right. I've been a barrel of laughs. I'm just glad I could come up here and help you all calm down. I tend to have that effect, and boy were you people stressed."

"It's been great having you here, Jane," Paul said warmly. "Seriously. And you're not leaving yet. We have three more days, and one of them includes a picnic, a boat, and most likely swimming in the harbor of Rock Island. It's pretty there, and the water is ten times warmer than it is here."

Jane looked genuinely pleased, and when I looked at Paul he was perfectly at ease.

And so it was decided. The next day was a sailing day. For better or worse, the five of us were going to be stuck on a boat for most of a day.

The rest of our evening was quiet and easy. The four of us talked long after Stephen had gone back to his room. Paul and Jane ended up next to each other on the couch while Issa and I pulled our chairs close enough that we could lean on one another. When the night finally ended, I was left alone with Jane as the others went off to bed.

"Do you want to stay? I mean, do you want to stay with me? I've always slept well next to you."

"No funny business?"

"I think we've both had enough funny business these last

few days."

"Were you two really fucking when we got back the other night?"

"Of course not. We'd finished at least a half hour earlier. We were just lying there naked. What about you? Did you really break in the apartment with Paul?"

"It was more of a kiss and a blow job. We looked around and we talked for a long time, but we hardly know each other."

"So, it was a getting-to-know-you blow job?"

"Exactly."

Jane followed me into my room and undressed without talking. We walked to the bathroom in our underwear and brushed our teeth together. I held the towel for her after she washed her face, and she turned out the light after we climbed into bed. We snuggled closely as the breeze from the open window shook the sill. I wrapped my arms around her and closed my eyes.

Chapter Twenty-One

The next morning Paul and Jane chatted as we packed bags and made sandwiches. Paul picked out a few bottles of good picnic wine while Issa and I found whatever leftover salads we had in the fridge and transferred them to Tupperware. Stephen changed clothes three times, and by the time the clouds had cleared, the five of us were riding into town—two to a bike—struggling not to fall over.

Abigail was, as always, calm, direct, and concise.

"Hey, New York, you sailing with these old-timers?" she asked when we sat down.

"Think I'm in good hands? I've never seen either one of them sail a boat."

"Couldn't say. Maybe I should get my rent up front before ya leave."

"We'll be just fine, Abigail," Paul said with a smile. "I've done this once or twice before."

"Well, don't bother the pots, and mind the bell buoys. It's windy out there."

She didn't sit down with us, but our waiter kept the fresh coffee coming and the morning felt full of possibilities.

"I'm glad we get to hang out today," Stephen said to me. The other three were in their own world, and Stephen and I had a brief moment to lean back and talk as we drank our coffee and looked out over the water.

"I feel like I haven't seen too much of you, even though you've been home." I knew it was because I had been ignoring him as much as I had been everyone else. Ignoring Stephen had at least been unintentional, but he was a casualty of all the shit going on in my head and I felt bad about it. I just wasn't sure what to say.

"Well, it's not my fault, you've been so busy."

"I know, man. I know. Have you been back to the cave?" I asked.

He shook his head as he poured far too much sugar into his espresso.

Jane was sitting between Paul and Issa, and despite what I kept expecting to be a somewhat awkward moment, they were all completely at ease. Every once in a while Paul put a hand on Jane's leg and Issa didn't seem to mind. I continued talking with Stephen as we ate, and before long we were finished and ready to head out to see what might be found on the open waters.

The sailboat was waiting for us on the dock, and the owner gave us a brief tour. It was a 26-foot boat with a small cabin below, a single mainsail, and a jib. It could be easily sailed by two people and it was manageable by one (as long as that one person wasn't me). The owner went out on his own for days at a time, and he was perfectly comfortable with Paul and Stephen's ability to keep us all safe and afloat. He showed them how everything worked while the rest of us made ourselves comfortable.

Jane was wearing light cotton drawstring pants with a matching bikini top. Issa had on shorts and a tank top, and they had hats on that looked likely to blow off if the wind picked up at all. I took off my shoes, rolled up my cargo pants and slid down onto the deck between them. Without realizing it they each grabbed a hand and I squeezed them both as the boys untied us and pushed us off from the dock.

Paul pulled up the sail as Stephen took the wheel, and before too long we were gliding out of the harbor on the cool Maine wind. We stayed close to the coastline of the island as we sailed out, and within an hour we passed the house on the rocky shore. We all waved to the porch and shouted out greetings. With each passing minute I felt more alive. The two women sitting next to me helped almost as much as the warm ocean breeze.

"This is the fucking life," Jane said as she leaned her head against my shoulder.

"Yes it is," Issa said as she pulled off her tank top and lay back on the deck of the boat. She was wearing a somewhat larger bikini top than Jane, but I found my eyes counting her freckles in spite of myself. Jane leaned in and whispered to me.

"Her tits are fucking awesome. I can't believe you get to see them."

"Quit it," I said poking her in the ribs. She looked at me with a knowing grin until I backed down.

"They're epic. You love them," she whispered again.

"What are you talking about over there?" Issa asked, sitting up on the deck.

"I was just saying it's almost time to open a bottle of wine," Jane replied without a pause. Paul was one step ahead of her, and two minutes later he handed us all plastic cups full of white wine.

"And what are we drinking this time, Paul?" I asked.

"This is a Sauvignon blanc from Washington State. It was made for picnics. And I brought the last four bottles."

Stephen and Paul navigated us along the coast as we drank our wine, until we moved off the north end of the island. The waves picked up just enough to toss us about, and we held onto the lines with one hand and our drinks with the other. We sailed north towards the next island, which was uninhabited and about half the size of ours. The boys maneuvered us into a small cove and dropped anchor in the calm waters sheltered by the rocks and trees.

With picnic basket in hand and our pants rolled to our knees, we waded through the shallow waters and up onto the rocky shore. Stephen lead the way through the scraggly trees along a nearly nonexistent path until we came to a high flat rock near the center of the island. We climbed up onto the plateau, set down our blanket, and began unpacking our lunch. We pulled out sandwiches, potato salad, and cheese, along with a bowl of olives and another bottle of wine. We sprawled out on the hot stone and ate slowly as the sun warmed our bodies and tanned our skins.

"Can we eat lunch like this every day?" Jane asked between bites of smoked salmon and chèvre on black bread.

"I am so down with that," Issa mumbled as she stuffed blue cheese into her mouth on a thick slice of pear. "A picnic every day, the hot sun on my body, and friends all around."

"I'll drink to that," Stephen cried as he grabbed Issa's glass of wine and finished off what was left.

"That was very not cool, little man," Issa scolded as she poured herself another.

"When in Rome," he said with a grin before jumping up and pulling off his shirt. "So, who's ready to go swimming?"

"I think the old people need to a wait a bit longer before jumping in the water," Paul told him. "But go, young man! Swim in the frigid water, and come back and tell us if you think we will all survive it."

Stephen jumped down off the rocks, and disappeared through the trees before anyone said a thing.

"You don't worry about him going off like that?" Jane asked him.

"He's fourteen and is less likely to kill himself on the rocks than I am. Some kids I wouldn't trust, but that one has a good head on his shoulders. He's nearly done cooking, and I wish I could say I had something to do with how well he turned out, but the truth is I got lucky.

"Besides," he continued as he leaned in towards Jane, "now I can steal kisses." He leaned in closer and kissed her on the mouth as both Issa and I turned our heads in mock embarrassment. For some reason it didn't even occur to me to be surprised. Issa leaned in and kissed me as well, and when no one else was looking, she whispered in my ear.

"If Stephen wasn't here, I could be talked into skinny dipping again."

"And now I want you. Just like that. Why do you do that to me?"

"Because it's way too easy. And also, because I still want you too."

"If we're not careful those two will be naked before he gets back."

"They're cute, aren't they?" she asked me.

"Cute like puppies. But it's strange. Does it ever bother you to see that?"

"I like seeing him happy. He's cute when he gets like that. Besides, if Paul is having dirty fun with Jane, he's usually up for dirty fun with me too. Nothing like a little sex to make you want a little more sex."

"I heard it was just a blow job."

"And I heard that she swallows."

"You definitely got more detail than I did." I was hit with a twinge of jealousy that sent a ripple right through my gut. Was it Jane and Paul that upset me or the fact that Issa knew more than I did?

"Sometimes I think you people are completely crazy," I said shaking my head.

"And the other times?"

"I think you might be brilliant. Well, brilliant and crazy."

She gave me a smile full of hope, and I felt my heart flutter a bit at the sight of her pink tongue and perfect teeth. We clinked our plastic cups together and turned back to the other two, who were not in fact naked or kissing each other.

We moved into a small circle on the rock as we shared wine and talked about nothing at all. We could see to all corners of the island from our high point and the ocean went on forever beyond the rocks and waves. Paul and I pulled off our shirts to get sun, and the four of us basked in the warmth of summer.

"So, are you two, like, dating now? How does that work?" Jane could always be relied on for tactful questions.

"I don't know. James, are we dating now? Can I be your girlfriend?"

"It's better than lover. Lover sounds like we're in an old novel."

"That's settled. He's my boyfriend. Anything else?" She was playful, but there was an edge to her voice that I loved. Jane just nodded and kept right on going.

"And do you have girlfriends as well?" she asked Paul.

"One. And the wife. I'm a simple man with simple tastes."

"Right. One wife, one girlfriend, and one ex-girlfriend of your wife's new boyfriend. Whatever that makes us."

"I think we're step-ex-partners-in-law. Or something like that. I'm not up on the latest terminology. It's hard to keep up out here on our island."

"And it works? I mean, just like that it, fucking works? Don't you ever get jealous and all those other things? I can barely stand watching James and Issa holding hands, and we broke up over a year ago. I think I'm less evolved."

"Of course we get jealous. We just don't always act on it. Unless it leads to super hot sex. Or possibly important conversations about self-care, honesty, and making sure everyone is getting their needs met."

"Jesus, you sound like a fucking therapist. Don't you ever just want to cheat? I mean, come on."

"Oh, I cheat all the time, I just don't tell Paul. Shhhhh." Issa held a finger to her mouth, grinning.

"She thinks I don't know, but I read her diary."

"I think I'm ready for a swim," Issa said, jumping up. "Anyone want to come join me?"

Paul decided they should both, in fact, go and check up on Stephen, and they left Jane and me alone on the rocks. I rolled over next to her and rubbed sunscreen onto her back until she let out a little moan of pleasure. I pressed my fingers harder into her warm muscles.

"All make sense now? Or do you still have more questions?"

"I'm sure I'll think of something else. Don't worry, you'll know. But in the meantime, that feels amazing," she whispered into her arm as she shook her head. "I think I love you."

I smiled, but didn't say a thing. Jane had a habit of loving me at very convenient times. When I finished she rolled over and looked up at me with her big blue eyes. All the New York tension and stress had vanished in the days she had been with us and she was prettier than I remembered; I suddenly wanted to do terrible, wonderful things to her. She reached a hand up and touched my face. I placed a hand next to her head and leaned in closely.

"Do you really have to leave?"

"I do. Why don't you come back with me? Even just for a few days. It's not really that far, and I bet everyone would love to see you."

"I don't know. I feel like I just started writing again. I haven't burned anything in days."

"Well, the invitation stands. New York misses you and so do I." She lay down on her back and looked up at the sky. She was so familiar it was hard not to fall back into old habits of affection.

"You are so fucking beautiful, sometimes I can't stand it."

"After seven years, you still think I'm beautiful?"

"What can I say? You just get better with age."

"Like cheese."

"I was thinking like wine, actually."

"Even after everything else?"

It was my turn to pause, because at the end of the day Jane doesn't often ask serious questions. I looked at her eyes and I remembered everything. The good, the bad, and the hungover. I could see her crying and laughing and all the time we spent together washed over me in a wave of emotion. For a brief moment I saw it all together as a tapestry of joys and sorrows, and they were woven so deeply together there was no way to take them apart.

The answer didn't require words.

When I kissed her, it was not gentle-sweet. I bit her bottom lip and pulled her head to me with a firm hand. She let out a small sigh as she wrapped her arms around me and her hot skin pressed into mine and we didn't stop. I pushed my fingers into her back as we kissed, and her hand on my leg was curious and fearless. Everything familiar rolled back in an instant.

There was almost no thinking involved as I tasted wine and olives on her breath, and I felt desire surge through my body without shame or guilt. When we finally stopped, she took a deep breath as she rested her forehead against mine.

"I want you," was all I said. She nodded and I kissed her again, but before long we had to pry ourselves away from each other for fear of being interrupted doing more than just kissing. We held hands as we walked down along the path, and I tried as hard as I could to forget the day before.

When we found the small beach where everyone was swimming, Stephen called out to us. Issa was sitting on Paul's shoulders in the water and they were chasing Stephen through the waves splashing him with four hands. The laughter was contagious, and we were in the ocean in seconds. The cold sent a chill through my body almost instantly, but within a few minutes I got used to it, and we splashed and played in the afternoon sun.

I offered Stephen my shoulders to even the score, and Jane crawled up onto a rock to watch the four of us try to topple each other over.

"Go faster," Stephen shouted, as I tried to move around behind Paul and Issa.

"It's rocky down there," I yelled, as I struggled to keep my balance. The wine didn't help, and I almost fell over a few times.

Paul and Issa turned just as we reached them and she and Stephen locked hands in a vicious battle. I grabbed Paul for balance as we played, and before too long he winked at me.

"One! Two! Three!" we yelled, before dumping them off our shoulders into the cold water and scurrying up onto the rock with Jane between us. Paul and I each leaned in and kissed a cheek without thinking, and we all sat laughing as the other two shook the water out of their hair and vowed their revenge with ominous tones and frightening stares.

We packed up the picnic before too long and decided some more sailing would do us good. Once again, the boys did all the work while I lay on the deck between Issa and Jane, and the afternoon passed as wonderfully as the morning. We sailed around the small island, caught some wind on the open sea, and sang some shanties at Stephen's request. By the time we returned to the island we were hot, exhausted, and completely content. We ate dinner at the café, as we were all too tired to cook, and just before we were about to head home I pulled Jane aside.

"I don't need to go home yet," I said quietly as I leaned in close. "If you're looking for a little company, that is."

For the first year of our relationship that was our phrase. We'd be at a party or out with some friends, and one of us would lean in whisper in the other's ear, "Looking for a little company?" It meant one thing, and we both knew what it was. We made so many exits on false pretenses that first year that our friends began to just roll their eyes and make rabbit ears as we walked out.

"Oh God yes," she said with a grin. "Let's check with them and then get the hell upstairs."

We huddled together with Paul and Issa, and they were perfectly comfortable with the suggestion that I might spend the night at the apartment with Jane. They kissed us both as they climbed onto their bikes, and all three of them waved as they rode off into the darkening night. I watched as they rolled away, and at the last minute Issa turned to me with a wink.

I had Jane's bikini top off before she got in the door. We kissed as she locked it behind me, and I pushed her against the wall and pressed my body against hers. Her hand reached down to my belt and she pulled it off as I lost my shirt. This was familiar.

"What do you want?" she whispered in my ear as I pulled open the string to her pants. There was only one answer to that question.

"I want to fuck you," I growled as I kissed her again.

"Are you sure you don't want to make love?" she asked, pushing me back and lowering her eyes. I turned her around and pulled her head back by her hair. One hand pinched a nipple between strong fingers as the other slid down her stomach beneath everything she had on. She moaned when I touched her clit, and I bit her ear between breaths.

"I'm sure," I said as I pressed against her from behind. She grabbed my hand and pulled me to the bed, and moments later there was no doubt at all about what I wanted to do. When I slid inside her, it was so familiar I nearly laughed. Her body moved exactly as I remembered, and we fit in all the right ways. She bit me and I slapped her, and she called me names until I fucked her as hard as she needed.

"Are you jealous about me and Paul?" she asked, looking up into my eyes.

"Are you jealous about Issa?"

"How many times have you fucked her?" She was groaning

and her hand moved between her legs as she waited for my answer.

"Not enough," I said with a thrust. Without warning my hand moved to her throat and her eyes opened wide as I squeezed.

"Did you really let Paul come in your mouth?"

When she didn't answer I squeezed harder and pulled all the way out of her body. She moaned and struggled to push back down around me, but I held her firmly. She knew I would wait.

"Yes," she finally moaned as I slammed back inside her.

We spent hours that night in bed, on the floor, and on the easy chair by the window overlooking the bay. We fucked and kissed, and even made love as the night passed us by. We let out every hidden emotion, and fought one another over and over again. Her body worked just as I remembered it. This wasn't about getting reacquainted; it was about needing and wanting in ways I had nearly forgotten. It was about nails and teeth and taking what we wanted as much as we gave. Our bodies shook and trembled as muscle memory took over, and we pushed them to utter exhaustion.

We fell asleep just before the sun rose, and we slept late into the morning. We showered together for the first time in years, and when we finally pulled on our clothes it was at the demand of our stomachs.

Abigail was friendly as always when we stumbled downstairs for breakfast, and the coffee was strong and delicious. The morning was quiet as we lost the sleep from our eyes, and the awkwardness I kept expecting never appeared. We smiled at each other and ate, and every once in a while we burst into laughter as we remembered the night before.

Chapter Twenty-Two

I left Jane in her new room in the late afternoon and made my way back home. It was hot and bright, and the closer I got, the more I wondered if explanations were needed. When I got back to the house it was quiet and empty. Paul and Stephen were out, and the kitchen was dark. It wasn't until I walked out onto the porch that I saw Issa reading on the couch.

"Hey handsome, you have a good night?"

I nodded and sat down next to her. Her eyes moved back to her book and I wasn't sure if I was interrupting.

"Is there a protocol for how much I'm supposed to say in these situations?"

"Well, you can start by asking me how much I want to know."

"Once again, you have a simple, yet elegant answer to my stupid question. So, how much do you want to know?"

"Did you fuck her?"

"Yup."

"That's all. Not that I'm not curious, but right now I don't need anything else. Jane is great, but I'm still getting used to the fact that my husband is seeing her, and now my boyfriend is too, and I'm not ready to listen."

"Issa, I'm not going to replace you. I mean, it's not like she's..."

"James, I didn't ask you to justify anything. I'm just saying that I'm not ready right now. I can deal with it fine, but right now I'm feeling fragile. You don't have to fix me."

I wondered what my life would have been like if I had known that years ago. I had spent more time trying to fix people—trying to make them happier—than was good for anyone. If I couldn't make it better, then I had to deal with the hard parts, but maybe that was okay too.

"Do you mind if I write while you're reading?"

"Go right ahead."

I returned a minute later with my notebook, and sat back on the couch next to her. I opened to a blank page and tried to think of what I had to say.

There's a redhead sitting next to me who is going to keep me up at night.

I looked over at her, but once again she was lost in her book.

Her eyes are green and she has freckles that cover her breasts in patterns an artist couldn't dream up. She moans when I kiss her ear and she sighs when I hold her tightly.

I saw a flicker of eye movement.

Sometimes when I'm with her I wonder what it would be like to kiss every inch of her body. I can describe it in vivid details, but I'll start with her toes. I'll move to her ankle and then her calf, and if she wiggles I'll have to tie her to the bed. When I get to her thighs I'll wait longer and longer between each kiss and...

"That is totally not fair. I'm trying to sit here reading and you're distracting me."

"Issa," I said with horror. "Were you reading over my shoulder? That is completely rude."

"Well, if you weren't writing dirty things then maybe I wouldn't have to. You just need to be the center of attention, don't you?'

"Maybe," I said. "I could go write over there if you want."

"And now you're pouting as well. Such a big boy."

"You are impossible. And I love you."

"I'm glad that's settled. Why don't you sit still so I can lie down in your lap and read my book? If you need something to do, trying watching the waves. They're pretty this time of day."

She lay down on her back and kicked her bare feet up on the edge of the couch. She held the book in front of her and for a long time we didn't move at all. I stared out over the water, and I let my mind drift through the last few weeks of my life. When I caught up to the present, I was suddenly aware that I had no idea what was next.

"Are you going to leave when Jane does tomorrow?" Issa interrupted my thoughts with the question I was about to ask myself.

"Why would I do that?"

"I don't know. You were together for so long, and now it looks like it might happen again, and I just thought you might want to get back to your life."

"This is my life."

"Sort of."

"New York is far away, and I don't like the idea of having to come all the way up here to visit you."

"Could I come visit you?" she asked, sitting up on the couch. "I haven't been to New York in years. We could get a hotel and you could show me all the places you love. We could go everywhere that Abigail has mentioned, and I could write her postcards with photos of the bars and parks. We could take a horse and carriage ride through the park and we could fuck on a rooftop."

"It sounds like a dream."

"I didn't expect you to stay here forever. Don't you need to work someday too?"

"I'm a writer. I'm always working."

"You know what I mean."

The idea of trying to write for a living once more suddenly filled me with more curiosity than dread. I had been so focused on my own emotional baggage that I hadn't really thought about my life. Could I just pack up and go? My apartment was waiting for me. I had a bartending job if I wanted it, and once my mind stopped fucking with me, I had another story in me to tell.

"It suddenly feels like you're already gone."

I leaned down and kissed her forehead. And then I kissed her nose and finally her lips. She pulled me closer and our kiss lasted. I didn't want to let her go, and I didn't want to go anywhere, let alone home.

"I hadn't even thought about leaving until yesterday, and now I can't get it out of my mind. I want to write something real, and for some reason I think I need to be back in New York to do that."

"You've been writing here the whole time. I've never seen you not writing."

"I don't know if you can call it that. It was more like mental masturbation."

"There's nothing wrong with that."

The truth was I was scared of staying as much as I was of leaving. I was falling for Issa harder than I could have imagined, and yet where could it go? I was sharing her with a man I adored, but I couldn't stay there forever. I would begin to want more of her time and I'd want nights and days.

"We don't have to break up just because you're leaving, you know."

"I never said I was leaving."

"You didn't have to. Most of my relationships have been long distance. I'll visit and you can visit us too. We can write dirty letters and call each other when they feel too slow. It doesn't have to be over."

I kissed her and then kissed her again. Breaking up was the last thing I wanted, and I planned on kissing her until she knew it. When we finally sat up it was with a sigh.

"I'm going to miss you," I said.

"You better fucking miss me. But I suppose I'll survive. I might have to make a trip to Florence, though. I get bored on my own."

"You're not doing that without me."

"Hey, you don't own me."

"Not for lack of trying."

We didn't get off the couch for the rest of the afternoon and when Jane and Paul arrived in the evening we were starving. The five of us ate in the kitchen and our meal was slow and easy. We talked and laughed until we stumbled out onto the porch one last time.

"So, I hear our house is going to return to its normal size by tomorrow night."

Paul was smoking in his chair and Stephen was curled up with a book trying to ignore the rest of us.

"I'm going to miss this," I said.

"We're going to miss you too."

"Can't you stay another week?" Stephen asked, looking up.

"If I wait until next week I'll have to wait a whole other month until I get my room back. And I need to get back to work. It's been incredibly kind of you to let me stay here, but somewhere in the world I have bills to pay."

Issa leaned on my shoulder and took my hand in hers. Home was exciting, but leaving her was not.

"Do you two want to stay at the café tonight?" Jane asked. "I can crash in your room and meet you at the ferry in the morning."

I looked back and forth between her and Paul. He looked at Issa, she looked at Jane, and without a word we somehow figured things out.

"We'd love that, Jane. Thank you," Issa said. Stephen was back in his book and there was nothing else to decide. I was leaving, but first, I had one last night with Issa. I had one last night on the island, and one last night to make sure everything stayed with me.

It was late when we got to the café and the lights were off. I unlocked the door and we climbed the stairs quietly. Jane had left the window open and it was wonderfully cool in the room.

"Well, this feels familiar," Issa said, turning to kiss me.

"It does bring back some memories."

"Are you sad it's just the two of us?"

"The only thing I'm sad about is how long it's going to be until I see you again. How about you come visit tomorrow?"

"How about in two weeks?"

I kissed her again and pulled her to me. My hands slipped up her back beneath her shirt and she closed her eyes as she sat down on my lap. I took my time with her buttons and she did the same with mine. I folded her shirt and she tossed mine to the floor. We were naked within minutes and her body was warm against my own.

"Do you think you'll ever play with another man again?" she asked as I moved down her body. I kissed her breasts, taking each nipple between my teeth, and then moved down to her stomach.

"I don't know. Maybe if you were there."

"I can't believe I got to watch you suck him off."

"For a whole thirty seconds," I said before I pressed my lips to her thigh.

"It was super hot."

When my mouth opened between her legs she stopped talking. I pressed my tongue inside her followed quickly by my fingers. I wanted to swallow her whole and take her with me when I left. I wanted to climb inside her and never lose her touch.

"Come here," she whispered as she pulled me up to her mouth. Her kiss was warm and tasted like sex. It was long and slow and somewhere in the middle of it, I was inside her. We moved together for a long time without a word. She climbed on top of me and we both watched as she rubbed her body against mine. She teased us both with her hands and fingers, and each time I slid inside her we moaned into the night wind.

We came and we cried as we held each other. She kissed my eyes and I tasted her tears. We pulled a blanket up over us, but we never stopped moving. Each time I thought we were done one of us shifted a knee or uttered a word that reminded our bodies of what they wanted. She brought me back to life over and over again, and each time she shook around me I found myself laughing with joy.

We kissed and dozed until the sun came up. I wrapped my arms around her and told her I loved her once more. We closed our eyes and slept until someone knocked on the door to tell us it was time for breakfast.

Paul, Stephen, and Jane were sitting at a large round table on the patio when we came down. Jane was back to wearing black and her bags were neatly packed by her chair. My suitcase had mostly survived the trip, but it was more sorrowful than romantic. When Abigail brought our coffees out she sat down and joined us for a while.

"So, New York," she said.

"I love it up here, but I can't seem to write all that much. All that comes out are bars and crowded subways."

"Ayuh. That's about right."

"How is that about right, Abigail? I should be writing about the ocean and the seagulls. I should be writing about you and the boats in the harbor."

"Go to the Oyster Bar for me when you're home."

"Abigail, what is it about you and New York? "

She leaned back in her chair and looked out over the

bay. I wasn't sure if she heard me, but I didn't want to ask again. She was never invasive, but she asked about landmarks that were more like fantasy than anything else. It was always bars and restaurants, and her eagerness was sincere and powerful all at the same time. No one else said a word.

"Two years of college, and I never went back. The city ate me up and spat me out again, and here I am. I remember the names and the streets. I remember the long dark walks I used to take, looking up at the buildings wishing there were stars. Sometimes the names are all I remember."

I looked at her, but didn't find words. For weeks I had answered her questions, and each one was another opportunity to think about the city I loved. I could imagine her as a young woman walking through Grand Central to get a perfect cocktail along with oysters so cold and delicious they melted in your mouth. I could see her in the East Village or in Chinatown for dim sum. I almost wished I still had my pages so I could show her what I'd written. I wanted her to sit and read my words to see just where her questions had taken me, but there was nothing I could do. The words were gone.

"What do you think I'll write about when I'm home?"

"I imagine when you're home you'll write about the island."

"It's about time you started writing about us," Stephen added. "What's the point of living with a writer if they don't put you in a story?"

"I'll see what I can do," I told him. "Abigail, I think I'm going to miss you,"

She didn't smile, but her face was warm and friendly. She got up after a while and took the empty glasses off a nearby table.

"You'll get used to it," she said. She gave me a hug and then she was gone.

"Are you two ready? We don't want to miss the ferry." Paul was standing, and suddenly it was very real.

I held Issa's hand as we walked down to the dock, and she kissed me as we waited to board. Her hair was tied back and even though we had barely slept at all she was as lovely as ever.

"I'll see you soon," I managed to say.

"James, I love you."

"I love you too."

"I also love you, James. In a kind of manly way, though. But I will miss you. Come back any time you like." Paul gave me a bear hug that cracked my back. I hugged Stephen as well, and he waved to us as Jane and I walked up onto the ferry. The three of them stood arm in arm as we drifted out into the harbor, and we watched them until they were too small to see on the horizon.

"I thought you were happy here," Jane said when we were finally alone. "You're writing and you have an amazing girlfriend and a great husband-in-law. Why would you want to leave?"

"Because you're right. I'm not writing; I'm burning things and trying to forget. What's the point if I'm not writing something for someone? I don't even mean someone specific. I just mean that books are meant to be read, and I'm not writing a book."

"Did you know that I never unwrapped the paintings from our apartment? They're in storage with the paper and sheets still covering them because every time I thought about looking at them I was reminded of you. And it was just too much."

"At least we're both unstable."

"Oh, I'm way more normal than you are. But what about us? I mean, where do we go from here?"

"Well, I assumed we'd take the train together. For starters."

"And then?"

"Maybe a quickie in the bathroom?"

"You're such a romantic. Seriously though. Are we going to try something?"

"Do we need to sort that out now? I don't know what I'm going to do for work, I barely have a place to live, and I have no idea what's going to happen with me and Issa. Have you and Paul talked about it?"

"Me and Paul had fun this week. But it was just fun. I like him, and I think he likes me too, but we're not pining away for each other. If we see each other again we do, but I don't think either one of us is going to lose any sleep over it."

"Do you think you could do it?" I asked.

"What, live on an island and drink wine by the case?"

"Have two boyfriends."

"That's not what you're asking. What you mean is could I be with you if you're still with Issa. You're asking if I'm going to feel like she's always in the room. You want to know if I can be with you and not try to ruin everything else."

"Sure. I could have meant that."

"I don't know. Do we need to sort it out now?"

It was my turn to laugh. If I had learned anything on the island it was patience.

Jane and I sat next to each on the bus, and then the train. The closer we got to New York the more excited I became. Returning home with her beside me was the last thing I had ever expected, but somehow we didn't take up the same space. Our lives were intertwined, but more than ever before we had our own boundaries. I knew where she ended and I began, and it was a new sensation that left me content.

"Are you going back to our apartment?"

"It hasn't been our apartment in over a year, Jane."

"I can't call it Mike's apartment. I love Mike, but if anything, it's yours."

"My subletter is there through the end of the month. So I think I'm on the futon in the living room until he's out."

"You could always come stay with me."

"This is going to confuse the hell out of people."

I looked out the window at the passing landscape, but there

was nothing else to say. We hadn't decided on a thing and that was okay. As the towns grew more urban I began to think back to my weeks on the island, and for a moment I missed Issa with all my heart. I longed for the porch and the comfort of familiar habits. I wanted to walk the rocks with Stephen, and I wanted to laugh with Paul in the kitchen. I wanted wines I couldn't pronounce and a cold wind blowing through the window.

The longing passed quickly though and was replaced with something new. The island wasn't going anywhere, and there were already plans for a visit. I would see Issa again, and I'd write to her in between. She made me promise to send her a letter each week, and she demanded they be dirty. I left her with my vivid description of our morning with Sebastien and there would be more.

Penn Station was as crowded and loud as ever, but it felt good to have people around me. They rarely looked up from their phones as they pushed their way through the piles of luggage, and Jane and I were no different. We jumped on the subway together, but a few stops later I kissed her goodbye and stepped off onto the platform.

"I'll see you soon," she said before the doors closed.

No one was home when I walked in. I sat down on my old couch and put my feet up on the coffee table. My bedroom was full of a stranger's things, but the place was the same. Mike's bar was set up impeccably, and his books were alphabetized on the shelf. The rug Jane and I had bought at ABC Carpet was still in the center of the room and the sound of traffic out the window was strangely comforting. I was instantly reminded of Abigail's questions and the smell of coffee that came from her kitchen.

I pulled my phone out of my bag for the first time in a month, and I wrote a text to Suzanne. *Up for a drink tonight?*

I pulled my laptop out from the drawer below my feet, opened it, and turned the power on. I started a new document and smiled as memories came rushing back. I had only just begun to understand how things end, so for one last time I went back to the beginning.

I've always hated endings.

I don't finish books, I walk out of movies before I'm disappointed, and when it comes to relationships I'm even worse. I like to think it's merely a problem of habit, but in fact, I get scared. It's not my fear of being alone that keeps me there, but rather my overwhelming aversion to conflict. For years I convinced myself it was an evolutionary trait that must have somehow let my ancestors survive cold winter nights in their fur lined caves without getting into fights. The truth is that other people's unhappiness is often more than I can handle.

Which brings us to Jane.

Acknowledgements

There are many people who made this book possible in a thousand different ways.

My thanks go out to my dear friends Sam and Alissa, Mandy and Rob, J. Scott Grand, Dorothy Darker, The Dirty Gentleman, John, Kate, Amanda and Jack Stratton, who all supported me in getting these words down on paper. Also the whole Downtown Dirty Writing Roundtable, who listened to me read over the din of the bar after far too many manhattans. Frank and Diane were some of my first readers and gave me invaluable feedback. Many thanks to Tara for her proofreading skills, and of course my editor Rose Fox who changed this from a jumble of thoughts to a real book.

And to my family and friends who support me even in my most bizarre endeavours, a huge thank you. Especially my wife Laura Beth, who always encourages me no matter how ridiculous a plan I might hatch.

About the Author

Guy New York is an author, designer, and degenerate who spends most his time either writing about sex or having it. Sometimes he does both at the same time, much to the chagrin of his partners.

He is the creator of the blog Quickies in New York, which has been featured in Playboy Espanol, Violet Blue's Tiny Nibbles, and Fleshbot, among many others. In 2011 he and his partner in crime, The Dirty Gentleman, were voted #1 on Between My Sheet's list of the top 100 sex bloggers.

He has published numerous short stories, including *Love & Kink, Hana*, and *Winter to Spring*. This is his first novel.

You can follow Guy on twitter @quickiesnewyork and you can read his short stories (and view photos by The Dirty Gentleman) on his blog www.quickienewyork.com.